RAY
FAREWELL SUMMER

"[A] sequel long overdue."
San Jose Mercury News

"American literary icon Ray Bradbury has finally published the long-awaited sequel to his now classic novel,
Dandelion Wine. . . . The edgier *Farewell Summer* is
about a war between children and old people. . . .
Beautiful imagery and well-crafted prose. . . . This
is a darker, tougher Doug who is just beginning
to understand that those childhood days are not
going to last forever."
Chicago Sun-Times

"Charming and heartwarming, a coming-of-age story and
a nostalgic trip into a vanished Midwestern world.
Beneath the surface antics, however, lurks an undercur-
rent of existential angst—of the brevity and uncertainty of
life and the inevitability of death. If anything, the book
recalls Mark Twain's *The Adventures of Tom Sawyer* and
The Adventures of Huckleberry Finn, in which young
boys find themselves growing up in a world characterized
by complicated power struggles, oppression of the weak
by the strong, and strange concepts of morality. . . . Bradbury is one of the most prolific and celebrated fiction
writers of our time. . . . Judging from his latest book, he
retains, even in old age, a youthful spirit."
Nashville Tennessean

"Bradbury constructs a lovely fable."
Contra Costa Times

"Ray Bradbury has come full circle. . . . Bradbury fans will love the comic and wistful fable . . . an affirmation that their beloved storyteller can still write powerfully and poetically. . . . Hilarious. . . . A work that Mark Twain might have written had he and Tom Sawyer both lived in the 20th century. Bradbury demonstrates anew the power to convey wisdom in a few well-chosen words and images. . . . An elegant and concise work that should be sipped slowly and savored."

Columbus Dispatch

"Fifty years ago Ray Bradbury published one of the most beloved novels in 20th century American literature. . . . In *Farewell Summer*, an earthier novel of more concentrated scope than its predecessor, Bradbury takes up [the] story where it left off. . . . In terms of style and panache, the old wizard is still as full of joyful ambition as when he first began writing professionally."

Virginian Pilot

"In *Farewell Summer,* life pounces. . . . This novel distills youth to its ravenous essence. . . . Whereas *Dandelion Wine* captured childhood itself, *Farewell Summer* is a story of the changes that life and love bring. . . . In *Farewell Summer*, Bradbury argues for us all to leap into life with such abandon, because autumn's own red-golden glory can't be kept at bay forever."

Los Angeles Times Book Reviews

"Bradbury has a style all his own, much imitated but never matched."

Portland Oregonian

"Ray Bradbury's lovely new sequel to his 1957 *Dandelion Wine*. . . . The older Bradbury conserves his resources and aims his thunderbolts with more precision and wisdom. . . . It is impossible and irrelevant to classify it as better or worse. It is simply a different vintage of the same vineyard. . . . Vibrant . . . imaginative; Bradbury is incapable of being otherwise. But the joy is muted and measured, almost elegiac, tainted with the unspoken knowledge that all things, including us, must pass. . . . [Bradbury is] one of the few living geniuses of American letters."
South Florida Sun-Sentinel

"*Farewell Summer* takes place in that most rarified of places, Bradburyland, a place of lyric enchantment that readers have been visiting for more than 60 years. Bradbury is . . . still writing in a way that nobody else has ever matched. This is Bradbury in full ecstatic mode . . . ripe and delicious. . . . In a hard, cynical time, Ray Bradbury remains Ray Bradbury—an ardent romantic, a poet, a believer. Lots of writers love words, but few of them love life. Ray Bradbury loves both."
Palm Beach Post

"Poignant, wise. . . . Bradbury evokes the rhythms of a long-gone smalltown America with short, swift chapters that build to a lyrical meditation on aging and death. . . . Bradbury's mature but fresh return to his beloved early writing conveys a depth of feeling."
Publishers Weekly

"Ray Bradbury has accomplished what very few artists do . . . He has changed us."
Boston Sunday Globe

Books by Ray Bradbury

FAREWELL SUMMER

Ray Bradbury

HARPER

An Imprint of HarperCollinsPublishers

This book is a work of fiction. The characters, incidents, and dialogue are drawn from the author's imagination and are not to be construed as real. Any resemblance to actual events or persons, living or dead, is entirely coincidental.

HARPER

An Imprint of HarperCollins*Publishers*
10 East 53rd Street
New York, New York 10022-5299

Copyright © 2006 by Ray Bradbury
Interior photograph by Angelo Cavalli/Getty Images
ISBN: 978-0-06-113155-4
ISBN-10: 0-06-113155-5

First Harper paperback printing: November 2007
First William Morrow special printing: October 2006
First William Morrow hardcover printing: October 2006

Printed in the United States of America.

Visit Harper paperbacks on the World Wide Web at
www.harpercollins.com

10 9 8 7 6 5 4

With love to John Huff,
alive many years after
Dandelion Wine

Contents

FAREWELL
SUMMER

I.

ALMOST ANTIETAM

CHAPTER

One

THERE ARE THOSE DAYS WHICH SEEM A TAKING in of breath which, held, suspends the whole earth in its waiting. Some summers refuse to end.

So along the road those flowers spread that, when touched, give down a shower of autumn rust. By every path it looks as if a ruined circus had passed and loosed a trail of ancient iron at every turning of a wheel. The rust was laid out everywhere, strewn under trees and by river-banks and near the tracks themselves where once a locomotive had gone but went no more. So flowered flakes and railroad track together turned to moulderings upon the rim of autumn.

"Look, Doug," said Grandpa, driving into town from the farm. Behind them in the Kissel Kar were six large pumpkins picked fresh from the patch. "See those flowers?"

"Yes, sir."

"Farewell summer, Doug. That's the name of those flowers. Feel the air? August come back. Farewell summer."

"Boy," said Doug, "that's a sad name."

Grandma stepped into her pantry and felt the wind blowing from the west. The yeast was rising in the bowl, a sumptuous head, the head of an alien rising from the yield of other years. She touched the swell beneath the muslin cap. It was the earth on the morn before the arrival of Adam. It was the morn after the marriage of Eve to that stranger in the garden bed.

Grandma looked out the window at the way the sunlight lay across the yard and filled the apple trees with gold and echoed the same words:

"Farewell summer. Here it is, October 1st. Temperature's 82. Season just can't let go. The dogs are out under the trees. The leaves won't turn. A body would like to cry and laughs instead. Get up to the attic, Doug, and let the mad maiden aunt out of the secret room."

"*Is* there a mad maiden aunt in the attic?" asked Doug.

"No, but there should be."

Clouds passed over the lawn. And when the sun came out, in the pantry, Grandma almost whispered, *Summer, farewell.*

On the front porch, Doug stood beside his grandfather, hoping to borrow some of that far sight, beyond the hills, some of the wanting to cry, some of the ancient joy. The smell of pipe tobacco and Tiger shaving tonic had to suffice. A top spun in his chest, now light, now dark, now moving his tongue with laughter, now filling his eyes with salt water.

He surveyed the lake of grass below, all the dandelions gone, a touch of rust in the trees, and the smell of Egypt blowing from the far east.

"Think I'll go eat me a doughnut and take me a nap," Doug said.

CHAPTER

Two

LAID OUT IN HIS BED AT HIS OWN HOUSE NEXT door with a powdered-sugar moustache on his upper lip, Doug contemplated sleep, which lurked around in his head and gently covered him with darkness.

A long way off, a band played a strange slow tune, full of muted brass and muffled drums.

Doug listened.

It was as if the faraway band had come out of a cave into full sunlight. Somewhere a mob of irritable blackbirds soared to become piccolos.

"A parade!" whispered Doug, and leapt out of bed, shaking away sleep and sugar.

The music got louder, slower, deeper, like an immense storm cloud full of lightning, darkening rooftops.

At the window, Douglas blinked.

For there on the lawn, lifting a trombone, was Charlie Woodman, his best friend at school, and Will Arno, Charlie's pal, raising a trumpet, and Mr. Wyneski, the town barber, with a boa-constrictor tuba and—wait!

Doug turned and ran through the house.

He stepped out on the porch.

Down among the band stood Grandpa with a French horn, Grandma with a tambourine, his brother Tom with a kazoo.

Everyone yelled, everyone laughed.

"Hey," cried Doug. "What day is this?"

"Why," Grandma cried, "*your* day, Doug!"

"Fireworks tonight. The excursion boat's waiting!"

"For a *picnic*?"

"Trip's more like it." Mr. Wyneski crammed on his corn-flake-cereal straw hat. "Listen!"

The sound of a far boat wailed up from the lake shore.

"March!"

Grandma shook her tambourine, Tom thrummed his kazoo, and the bright mob drew Doug off along the street with a dog pack yipping at their heels. Downtown, someone threw a torn telephone book off the Green Town Hotel roof. When the confetti hit the bricks the parade was gone.

At the lake shore fog moved on the water.

Far out, he could hear a foghorn's mournful wail.

And a pure white boat loomed out of the fog and nudged the pier.

Doug stared. "How come that boat's got no *name*?"

The ship's whistle shrieked. The crowd swarmed, shoving Douglas to the gangplank.

"You *first,* Doug!"

The band dropped a ton of brass and ten pounds of chimes with "For He's a Jolly Good Fellow," as they thrust him on the deck, then leapt back on the dock.

Wham!

The gangplank fell.

The people weren't trapped on land, no.

He was trapped on water.

The steamboat shrieked away from the dock. The band played "Columbia, Gem of the Ocean."

"Goodbye, Douglas," cried the town librarians.

"So long," whispered everyone.

Douglas stared around at the picnic put by in wicker hampers on the deck and remembered a museum where he had once seen an Egyptian tomb with toys and clumps of withered fruit placed around a small carved boat. It flared like a gunpowder flash.

"So long, Doug, so long . . ." Ladies lifted their handkerchiefs, men waved straw hats.

And soon the ship was way out in the cold water with the fog wrapping it up so the band faded.

"Brave journey, boy."

And now he knew that if he searched he would find no captain, no crew as the ship's engines pumped belowdecks.

Numbly, he sensed that if he reached down to touch the prow he would find the ship's name, freshly painted:

FAREWELL SUMMER.

"Doug . . ." the voices called. "Oh, good-bye . . . oh, so long . . ."

And then the dock was empty, the parade gone as the ship blew its horn a last time and broke his heart so it fell from his eyes in tears as he cried all the names of his loves on shore.

"Grandma, Grandpa, Tom, *help*!"

Doug fell from bed, hot, cold, and weeping.

CHAPTER
Three

DOUG STOPPED CRYING.

He got up and went to the mirror to see what sadness looked like and there it was, colored all through his cheeks, and he reached to touch that other face, and it was cold.

Next door, baking bread filled the air with its late-afternoon aroma. He ran out across the yard and into his grandma's kitchen to watch her pull the lovely guts out of a chicken and then paused at a window to see Tom far up in his favorite apple tree trying to climb the sky.

Someone stood on the front porch, smoking his favorite pipe.

"Gramps, you're *here*! Boy, oh boy. The *house* is here. The *town's* here!"

"It seems *you're* here, too, boy."

"Yeah, oh, yeah."

The trees leaned their shadows on the lawn. Somewhere, the last lawnmower of summer shaved the years and left them in sweet mounds.

"Gramps, is—"

Douglas closed his eyes, and in the darkness said: "Is death being on a ship sailing and all your folks left back on the shore?"

Grandpa read a few clouds in the sky.

"That's about it, Doug. Why?"

Douglas eyed a high cloud passing that had never been that shape before and would never be that shape again.

"Say it, Gramps."

"Say what? Farewell summer?"

No, thought Douglas, *not if I can help it!*

And, in his head, the storm began.

CHAPTER

Four

THERE WAS A GREAT RUSHING SLIDING IRON
sound like a guillotine blade slicing the sky. The
blow fell. The town shuddered. But it was just
the wind from the north.

And down in the center of the ravine, the boys
listened for that great stroke of wind to come
again.

They stood on the creek-bank making water in
the cool sunlight and among them, preoccupied,
stood Douglas. They all smiled as they spelled
their names in the creek sand with the steaming

lemon water. CHARLIE, wrote one. WILL, another. And then: BO, PETE, SAM, HENRY, RALPH, and TOM.

Doug inscribed his initials with flourishes, took a deep breath, and added a postscript: WAR.

Tom squinted at the sand. "What?"

"War of course, dummy. War!"

"Who's the enemy?"

Douglas Spaulding glanced up at the green slopes above their great and secret ravine.

Instantly, like clockwork, in four ancient gray-flaked mansion houses, four old men, shaped from leaf-mold and yellowed dry wicker, showed their mummy faces from porches or in coffin-shaped windows.

"Them," whispered Doug. "Oh, *them*!"

Doug whirled and shrieked, "Charge!"

"Who do we kill?" said Tom.

CHAPTER
Five

ABOVE THE GREEN RAVINE, IN A DRY ROOM AT the top of an ancient house, old Braling leaned from a window like a thing from the attic, trembling. Below, the boys ran.

"God," he cried. "Make them stop their damned *laughing*!"

He clutched faintly at his chest as if he were a Swiss watchmaker concerned with keeping something running with that peculiar self-hypnosis he called prayer.

"Beat, *now;* one, *two*!"

Nights when he feared his heart might stop, he set a metronome ticking by his bed, so that his blood would continue to travel on toward dawn.

Footsteps scraped, a cane tip tapped, on the downstairs porch. That would be old Calvin C. Quartermain come to argue school board policy in the husking wicker chairs. Braling half fell down the stairs, emerging onto the porch.

"Quartermain!"

Calvin C. Quartermain sat like a wild mechanical toy, oversized, rusty, in a reed easy chair.

Braling laughed. "I *made* it!"

"Not forever," Quartermain observed.

"Hell," said Braling. "Some day they'll bury you in a California dried-fruit tin. Christ, what're those idiot boys up to?"

"Horsing around. *Listen*!"

"Bang!"

Douglas ran by the porch.

"Get off the lawn!" cried Braling.

Doug spun and aimed his cap-pistol.

"Bang!"

Braling, with a pale, wild look, cried, "Missed!"

"Bang!" Douglas jumped up the porch steps.

17

He saw two panicked moons in Braling's eyes.

"Bang! Your arm!"

"Who wants an *arm?*" Braling snorted.

"Bang! Your *heart*!"

"What?"

"Heart—bang!"

"Steady . . . One, *two!*" whispered the old man.

"Bang!"

"One, *two!*" Braling called to his hands clutching his ribs. "Christ! Metronome!"

"*What?*"

"Metronome!"

"Bang! You're dead!"

"One, two!" Braling gasped.

And dropped dead.

Douglas, cap-gun in hand, slipped and fell back down the steps onto the dry grass.

CHAPTER

Six

THE HOURS BURNED IN COLD WHITE WINTRY flashes, as people scuttled in and out of Braling's mansion, hoping against hope that he was Lazarus.

Calvin C. Quartermain careened about Braling's porch like the captain of a wrecked ship.

"Damn! I *saw* the boy's gun!"

"There's no bullet-hole," said Dr. Lieber, who'd been called.

"Shot dead, he was! Dead!"

The house grew silent as the people left, bearing away the husk that had been poor Braling. Calvin C. Quartermain abandoned the porch, mouth salivating.

"I'll find the killer, by God!"

Propelling himself with his cane, he turned a corner.

A cry, a concussion! "No, by God, no!" He flailed at the air and fell.

Some ladies rocking on the nearest porch leaned out. "Is that old Quartermain?"

"Oh, *he* can't be dead, too—*can* he?"

Quartermain's eyelids twitched.

Far off, he saw a bike, and a boy racing away.

Assassin, he thought. *Assassin!*

CHAPTER

Seven

WHEN DOUGLAS WALKED, HIS MIND RAN, WHEN he ran, his mind walked. The houses fell aside, the sky blazed.

At the rim of the ravine, he threw his cap-pistol far out over the gulf. An avalanche buried it. The echoes died.

Suddenly, he needed the gun again, to touch the shape of killing, like touching that wild old man.

Launching himself down the side of the ravine, Doug scrambled among the weeds, eyes wet, until he found the weapon. It smelled of gunpowder, fire, and darkness.

"Bang," he whispered, and climbed up to find his bike abandoned across the street from where old Braling had been killed. He led the bike away like a blind beast and at last got on and wobbled around the block, back toward the scene of awful death.

Turning a corner, he heard "No!" as his bike hit a nightmare scarecrow that was flung to the ground as he pumped off, wailing, staring back at one more murder strewn on the walk. Someone cried, "Is that old Quartermain?!"

"Can't be," Douglas moaned.

Braling fell, Quartermain fell. Up, down, up, down, two thin hatchets sunk in hard porch and sidewalk, frozen, never to rise.

Doug churned his bike through town. No mobs rushed after him.

It seemed the town did not even know that someone had been shot, another struck. The town poured tea and murmured, "Pass the sugar."

Doug slam-braked at his front porch. Was his mother waiting in tears, his father wielding the razor strop . . . ?

He opened the kitchen door.

"Hey. Long time no see." Mother kissed his brow. "They always come home when they're hungry."

"Funny," said Doug. "I'm not hungry at all."

CHAPTER

Eight

AT DINNER, THE FAMILY HEARD PEBBLES PING-
ing against the front door.

"Why," said Mother, "don't boys ever use the
bell?"

"In the last two hundred years," said Father,
"there is no recorded case in which *any* boy under fifteen ever got within ten feet of a doorbell.
You finished, young man?"

"Finished, sir!"

Douglas hit the front door like a bomb, skid-
ded, jumped back in time to catch the screen

before it slammed. Then he was off the porch
and there was Charlie Woodman on the lawn,
punching him great friendly punches.

"Doug! You did it! You shot Braling! Boy!"

"Not so loud, Charlie!"

"When do we shoot everyone on the school
board? For gosh sakes, they started school a
week early this year! They deserve to be shot.
My gosh, how'd you *do* it, Doug?"

"I said, 'Bang! You're dead!'"

"And Quartermain?!"

"Quartermain?"

"You broke his leg! Sure was your busy day,
Doug!"

"*I* didn't *break* no leg. My *bike* . . ."

"No, a *machine*! I heard old Cal screaming
when they lugged him home. 'Infernal machine!'
What *kind* of infernal machine, Doug?"

Somewhere in a corner of his mind, Doug saw
the bike fling Quartermain high, wheels spinning, while Douglas fled, the cry of Quartermain
following close.

"Doug, why didn't you crack *both* his legs
with your infernal machine?"

"What?"

"When do we see your device, Doug? Can you set it for the Death of a Thousand Slices?"

Doug examined Charlie's face, to see if he was joking, but Charlie's face was a pure church altar alive with holy light.

"Doug," he murmured. "Doug, boy, oh boy."

"Sure," said Douglas, warming to the altar glow. "Him against me, me against Quartermain and the whole darn school board, the town council—Mr. Bleak, Mr. Gray, all those dumb old men that live at the edge of the ravine."

"Can I watch you pick 'em off, Doug?"

"What? Sure. But we got to plan, got to have an army."

"Tonight, Doug?"

"Tomorrow . . ."

"No, *tonight*! Do or die. You be captain."

"General!"

"Sure, sure. I'll get the others. So they can hear it from the horse's mouth! Meet at the ravine bridge, eight o'clock! Boy!"

"Don't yell in the windows at those guys," said Doug. "Leave secret notes on their porches. That's an order!"

"Yeah!"

Charlie sped off, yelling. Douglas felt his heart drown in a fresh new summer. He felt the power growing in his head and arms and fists. All this in a day! From plain old C-minus student to full general!

Now, whose legs should be cracked next? Whose metronome stopped? He sucked in a trembling breath.

All the fiery-pink windows of the dying day shone upon this arch-criminal who walked in their brilliant gaze, half smile-scowling toward destiny, toward eight o'clock, toward the camptown gathering of the great Green Town Confederacy and everyone sitting by firelight singing, "Tenting tonight, tenting tonight, tenting on the old camp grounds . . ."

We'll sing that *one*, he thought, *three times*.

CHAPTER
Nine

UP IN THE ATTIC, DOUG AND TOM SET UP HEAD-
quarters. A turned-over box became the general's
desk; his aide-de-camp stood by, awaiting orders.

"Get out your pad, Tom."

"It's out."

"Ticonderoga pencil?"

"Ready."

"I got a list, Tom, for the Great Army of the
Republic. Write this down. There's Will and Sam
and Charlie and Bo and Pete and Henry and
Ralph. Oh, and you, Tom."

"How do we use the list, Doug?"

"We gotta find things for them to do. Time's running out. Right now we've gotta figure how many captains, how many lieutenants. One general. That's me."

"Make it good, Doug. Keep 'em busy."

"First three names, captains. The next three, lieutenants. Everybody else, spies."

"Spies, Doug?"

"I think that's the greatest thing. Guys like to creep around, watch things, and then come back and tell."

"Heck, I want to be one of those."

"Hold on. We'll make them *all* captains and lieutenants, make everyone happy, or we'll lose the war before it gets started. Some will do double-duty as spies."

"Okay, Doug, here's the list."

Doug scanned it. "Now we gotta figure the first sockdolager thing to do."

"Get the spies to tell you."

"Okay, Tom. But you're the most important spy. After the ravine meeting tonight . . ." Tom frowned, shook his head. "What?"

"Heck, Doug, the ravine's nice but I know a

better place. The graveyard. The sun'll be gone. It'll remind 'em if they're not careful, that's where we'll all wind up."

"Good thinking, Tom."

"Well, I'm gonna go spy and round up the guys. First the bridge, then the graveyard, yup?"

"Tom, you're really somethin'."

"Always was," said Tom. "Always was."

He jammed his pencil in his shirt pocket, stashed his nickel tablet in the waistband of his dungarees, and saluted his commander.

"Dismissed!"

And Tom ran.

CHAPTER
Ten

THE GREEN ACREAGE OF THE OLD CEMETERY WAS filled with stones and names on stones. Not only the names of the people earthed over with sod and flowers, but the names of seasons. Spring rain had written soft, unseen messages here. Summer sun had bleached granite. Autumn wind had softened the lettering. And snow had laid its cold hand on winter marble. But now what the seasons had to say was only a cool whisper in the trembling shade, the message of names: "TYSON! BOWMAN! STEVENS!"

Douglas leap-frogged TYSON, danced on BOWMAN, and circled STEVENS.

The graveyard was cool with old deaths, old stones grown in far Italian mountains to be shipped here to this green tunnel, under skies too bright in summer, too sad in winter.

Douglas stared. The entire territory swarmed with ancient terrors and dooms. The Great Army stood around him and he looked to see if the invisible webbed wings in the rushing air ran lost in the high elms and maples. And did they feel all that? Did they hear the autumn chestnuts raining in cat-soft thumpings on the mellow earth? But now all was the fixed blue lost twilight which sparked each stone with light specules where fresh yellow butterflies had once rested to dry their wings and now were gone.

Douglas led his suddenly disquieted mob into a further land of stillness and made them tie a bandanna over his eyes; his mouth, isolated, smiled all to itself.

Groping, he laid hands on a tombstone and played it like a harp, whispering.

"Jonathan Silks. 1920. Gunshot." Another: "Will Colby. 1921. Flu."

He turned blindly to touch deep-cut green moss names and rainy years, and old games played on lost Memorial Days while his aunts watered the grass with tears, their voices like windswept trees.

He named a thousand names, fixed ten thousand flowers, flashed ten million spades. "Pneumonia, gout, dyspepsia, TB. All of 'em taught," said Doug. "Taught to *learn* how to die. Pretty dumb lying here, doing nothing, yup?"

"Hey Doug," Charlie said, uneasily. "We met here to plan our army, not talk about dying. There's a billion years between now and Christmas. With all that time to fill, I got no time to die. I woke this morning and said to myself, 'Charlie, this is swell, *living*. Keep *doing* it!'"

"Charlie, that's how they *want* you to talk!"

"Am I wrinkly, Doug, and dog-pee yellow? Am I fourteen, Doug, or fifteen or twenty? *Am* I?"

"Charlie, you'll spoil everything!"

"I'm just not *worried*." Charlie beamed. "I figure everyone dies, but when it's *my* turn, I'll just say no thanks. Bo, you goin' to die someday? Pete?"

"Not me!"

"Me either!"

"See?" Charlie turned to Doug. "Nobody's dyin' like flies. Right now we'll just lie like hound-dogs in the shade. Cool off, Doug."

Douglas's hands fisted in his pockets, clutching dust, marbles, and a piece of white chalk. At any moment Charlie would run, the gang with him, yapping like dogs, to flop in deep grape-arbor twilight, not even swatting flies, eyes shut.

Douglas swiftly chalked their names, CHARLIE, TOM, PETE, BO, WILL, SAM, HENRY, AND RALPH, on the gravestones, then jumped back to let them spy themselves, so much chalk-dust on marble, flaking, as time blew by in the trees.

The boys stared for a long, long time, silent, their eyes moving over the strange shapes of chalk on the cold stone. Then, at last, there was the faintest exhalation of a whisper.

"Ain't going to die!" cried Will. "I'll fight!"

"Skeletons don't fight," said Douglas.

"No, sir!" Will lunged at the stone, erasing the chalk, tears springing to his eyes.

The other boys stood, frozen.

"Sure," Douglas said. "They'll teach us at

school, say, here's your heart, the thing you get attacks with! Show you bugs you can't *see*! Teach you to jump off buildings, stab people, fall and not move."

"No, sir," Sam gasped.

The great meadow of graveyard rippled under the last fingers of fading sunlight. Moths fluttered around them, and the sound of a graveyard creek ran over all their cold moonlit thoughts and gaspings as Douglas quietly finished: "Sure, none of us wants to just lie here and never play kick-the-can again. You want all that?"

"Heck no, Doug . . ."

"Then we *stop* it! We find out how our folks make us grow, teach us to lie, cheat, steal. War? Great! Murder? Swell! We'll never be so well off as we are right *now*! Grow up and you turn into burglars and get shot, or worse, *they* make you wear a coat and tie and stash you in the First National Bank behind brass bars! We gotta stand still! Stay the age we are. Grow up? Hah! All you do then is marry someone who *screams* at you! Well, do we fight back? Will you let me tell you how to run?"

"Gosh," said Charlie. "Yeah!"

"Then," said Doug, "talk to your body: Bones, not one more inch! Statues! Don't forget, Quartermain *owns* this graveyard. He makes money if we lie here, you and you and *you*! But we'll show him. And all those old men who own the town! Halloween's almost here and before then we got to sour their grapes! You wanna look like them? You know how they got that way? Well, they were all young once, but somewhere along the way, oh gosh, when they were thirty or forty or fifty, they chewed tobacco and phlegm-hocked up on themselves and that phlegm-hock turned all gummy and sticky and then the next thing you know there was spittle all over them and they began to look like, you know, you've seen, caterpillars turned into chrysalis, their darned skin hardened, and the young guys turned old, got trapped inside their shells, by God. Then they began to look like all those old guys. So, what you have is old men with young guys trapped inside them. Some year soon, maybe, their skin will crack and the old men will let the old young men out. But they won't be young anymore, they'll be a bunch of death's-head moths or, come to think of it, I think the old men are going to keep the young men inside them forever, so they're trapped in all that glue, always hoping to get free. It's pretty bad, isn't it? Pretty bad."

"Is that it, Doug?" said Tom.

"Yeah," said Pete. "You sure you know what you're talking about?"

"What Pete is trying to say is that we gotta know with precision, we gotta know what's accurate," said Bo.

"I'll say it again," said Doug. "You listen close. Tom, you taking this down?"

"Yup," said Tom, his pencil poised over his notepad. "Shoot."

They stood in the darkening shadows, in the smell of grass and leaves and old roses and cold stone and raised their heads, sniffling, and wiped their cheeks on their shirtsleeves.

"Okay, then," said Doug. "Let's go over it again. It's not enough just seeing these graves. We've got to sneak under open windows, listen, discover what those old geezers are sick with. Tom, go get the pumpkins out of Grandma's pantry. We're gonna have a contest, see which of us can carve the scariest pumpkin. One to look like old man Quartermain, one like Bleak, one like Gray. Light them up and put them out. Later tonight we start our first attack with the carved pumpkins. Okay?"

"Okay!" everyone shouted.

They leapt over WHYTE, WILLIAMS, and NEBB, jumped and vaulted SAMUELS and KELLER, screamed the iron gate wide, leaving the cold land behind them, lost sunlight, and the creek running forever below the hill. A host of gray moths followed them as far as the gate where Tom braked and stared at his brother accusingly.

"Doug, about those pumpkins. Gosh almighty, you're nuts!"

"What?" Doug stopped and turned back as the other boys ran on.

"It ain't enough. I mean, look what you've done. You've pushed the fellas too far, got 'em scared. Keep on with this sort of talk you're going to lose your army. You've got to do something that will put everything back together again. Find something for us to do or else everyone will go home and stay there, or go lie down with the dogs and sleep it off. Think of something, Doug. It's important."

Doug put his hands on his hips and stared at Tom. "Why do I got this feeling you're the general and I'm just a buck private?"

"What do you mean, Doug?"

"I mean here I am, almost fourteen, and you're twelve going on a hundred and ordering me around and telling me what to do. Are things so bad?"

"Bad, Doug? They're terrible. Look at all those guys running away. You better catch up and think of something between here and the middle of town. Reorganize the army. Give us something to do besides carving jack-o'-lanterns. Think, Doug, think."

"I'm thinking," said Doug, eyes shut.

"Well then, get going! Run, Doug, I'll catch up."

And Doug ran on.

CHAPTER
Eleven

ON THE WAY INTO TOWN, ON A STREET NEAR THE school stood the nickel emporium where all the sweet poisons hid in luscious traps.

Doug stopped, stared, and waited for Tom to catch up and then yelled, "Okay, gang, this way. In!"

Around him all the boys came to a halt because he said the name of the shop, which was pure magic.

Doug beckoned and they all gathered and followed, orderly, like a good army, into the shop.

Tom came last, smiling at Doug as if he knew something that nobody else knew.

Inside, honey lay sheathed in warm African chocolate. Plunged and captured in the amber treasure lay fresh Brazil nuts, almonds, and glazed clusters of snowy coconut. June butter and August wheat were clothed in dark sugars. All were crinkled in folded tin foil, then wrapped in red and blue papers that told the weight, ingredients, and manufacturer. In bright bouquets the candies lay, caramels to glue the teeth, licorice to blacken the heart, chewy wax bottles filled with sickening mint and strawberry sap, Tootsie Rolls to hold like cigars, red-tipped chalk-mint cigarettes for chill mornings when your breath smoked on the air.

The boys, in the middle of the shop, saw diamonds to crunch, fabulous liquors to swig. Persimmon-colored pop bottles swam, clinking softly, in the Nile waters of the refrigerated box, its water cold enough to cut your skin. Above, on glass shelves, lay cordwood piles of gingersnaps, macaroons, chocolate bits, vanilla wafers shaped like moons, and marshmallow dips, white surprises under black masquerades. All of this to coat the tongue, plaster the palate.

Doug pulled some nickels from his pocket and nodded at the boys.

One by one they chose from the sweet treasure, noses pressed against glass, breath misting the crystal vault.

Moments later, down the middle of the street they ran and soon stood on the edge of the ravine with the pop and candy.

Once they were all assembled, Doug nodded again and they started the trek down into the ravine. Above them, on the other side, stood the looming homes of the old men, casting dark shadows into the bright day. And above those, Doug saw, as he shielded his eyes, was the hulking carapace of the haunted house.

"I brought you here on purpose," said Doug.

Tom winked at him as he flipped the lid off his pop.

"You must learn to resist, so you can fight the good fight. Now," he cried, holding his bottle out. "Don't look so surprised. Pour!"

"My gosh!" Charlie Woodman slapped his brow. "That's good root beer, Doug. Mine's good Orange *Crush*!"

Doug turned his bottle upside down. The root

beer froth hissed out to join the clear stream rushing away to the lake. The others stared, the spectacle mirrored in each pair of eyes.

"You want to sweat Orange Crush?" Douglas grabbed Charlie's drink. "You want root beer spit, to be poisoned forever, to *never* get well? Once you're tall, you can't *un*-grow back, can't stab yourself with a pin and let the air out."

Solemnly, the martyrs tilted their bottles.

"Lucky crawfish." Charlie Woodman slung his bottle at a rock. They all threw their bottles, like Germans after a toast, the glass crashing in bright splinters.

They unwrapped the melting chocolate and butter chip and almond frivolities. Their teeth parted, their mouths watered. But their eyes looked to their general.

"I solemnly pledge from now on: no candy, no pop, no poison."

Douglas let his chocolate chunk drop like a corpse into the water, like a burial at sea.

Douglas wouldn't even let them lick their fingers.

Walking out of the ravine, they met a girl eating a vanilla ice cream cone. The boys stared, their tongues lolling. She took a cold dollop with her tongue. The boys blinked. She licked the cone and smiled. Perspiration broke out on a half dozen faces. One more lick, one more jut of that rare pink tongue, one more hint of cool vanilla ice cream and his army would revolt. Sucking in a deep breath, Douglas cried: "Git!"

The girl spun around and ran.

Douglas waited for the memory of the ice cream to fade, then said, quietly, "There's ice water at Grandma's. March!"

II.

SHILOH AND BEYOND

CHAPTER
Twelve

CALVIN C. QUARTERMAIN WAS AN EDIFICE AS tall, long, and as arrogant as his name.

He did not move, he stalked.

He did not see, he glared.

He spoke not, but fired his tongue, point-blank, at any target come to hand.

He orated, he pronounced, he praised not, but heaped scorn.

Right now he was busy shoving bacteria under the microscope of his gold-rimmed spectacles.

The bacteria were the boys, who deserved destruction. One boy, especially.

"A bike, sweet Christ, a damn blue bike! That's *all* it was!"

Quartermain bellowed, kicking his good leg.

"Bastards! Killed Braling! Now they're after *me*!"

A stout nurse trussed him like a cigar store Indian while Dr. Lieber set the leg.

"Christ! Damned fool. What was it Braling said about a *metronome*? Jesus!"

"Leg's broke, easy!"

"He needs more than a bike! A damned hellfire device won't kill *me*, no!"

The nurse shoved a pill in his mouth.

"Peace, Mr. C., peace."

CHAPTER
Thirteen

NIGHT, IN CALVIN C. QUARTERMAIN'S LEMON-sour house, and him in bed, discarded long ago, when his youth breeched the carapace, slid between his ribs, and left his shell to flake in the wind.

Quartermain twisted his head and the sounds of the summer night breathed through the air. Listening, he chewed on his hatred.

"God, strike down those bastard fiends with fire!"

Sweating cold, he thought: *Braling lost his*

brave fight to make them human, but I *will prevail. Christ, what's happening?*

He stared at the ceiling where gunpowder blew in a spontaneous combustion, all their lives exploded in one day at the end of an unbelievably late summer, a thing of weather and blind sky and the surprise miracle that he still lived, still breathed, amidst lunatic events. Christ! Who ran this parade and where was it going? God, stand alert! The drummer-boys are killing the captains.

"There must be others," he whispered to the open window. "Some who tonight feel as I do about these infidels!"

He could sense the shadows trembling out there, the other old rusted iron men hidden in their high towers, sipping thin gruels and snapping dog-biscuits. He would summon them with cries, his fever like heat-lightning across the sky.

"Telephone," gasped Quartermain. "Now, Calvin, line them up!"

There was a rustling in the dark yard. "*What?*" he whispered.

The boys clustered in the lightless ocean of grass below. Doug and Charlie, Will and Tom,

Bo, Henry, Sam, Ralph, and Pete all squinted up at the window of Quartermain's high bedroom.

In their hands they had three beautifully carved and terrible pumpkins. They carried them along the sidewalk below while their voices rose among the starlit trees, louder and louder: "The worms crawl in, the worms crawl out."

Quartermain turned each of his spotted papyrus hands into fists and clenched the telephone.

"Bleak!"

"Quartermain? My God, it's late!"

"Shut up! Did you hear about Braling?"

"I knew one day he'd get caught without his hourglass."

"This is no time for levity!"

"Oh, him and his damn clocks; I could hear him ticking across town. When you hold that tight to the edge of the grave, you should just jump in. Some boy with a cap-pistol means nothing. What can you do? Ban cap-pistols?"

"Bleak, I *need* you!"

"We all need each other."

"Braling was school board secretary. I'm *chairman*! The damn town's *teeming* with killers *in embryo*."

"My dear Quartermain," said Bleak dryly, "you remind me of the perceptive asylum keeper who claimed that his inmates were mad. You've only just discovered that boys are animals?"

"*Something* must be done!"

"*Life* will do it."

"The damned fools are outside my house singing a funeral dirge!"

"'The Worms Crawl In'? My favorite tune when I was a boy. Don't you remember being ten? Call their folks."

"Those fools? They'd just say, 'Leave the nasty old man alone.'"

"Why not pass a law to make everyone seventy-nine years old?" Bleak's grin ran along the telephone wires. "I've two dozen nephews who sweat icicles when I threaten to live forever. Wake up, Cal. We are a minority, like the dark African and the lost Hittite. We live in a country of the young. All we can do is wait until some of these sadists hit nineteen, then truck them off to war. Their crime? Being full up with orange juice and spring rain. Patience. Someday soon you'll see them wander by with winter in their hair. Sip your revenge quietly."

"Damn! Will you help?"

"If you mean can you count on my vote on the school board? Will I command Quartermain's Grand Army of Old Crocks? I'll leer from the sidelines, with an occasional vote thrown to you mad dogs. Shorten summer vacations, trim Christmas holidays, cancel the Spring Kite Festival—that's what you plan, yes?"

"I'm a lunatic, then?!"

"No, a student-come-lately. I learned at fifty I had joined the army of unwanted men. We are not quite Africans, Quartermain, or heathen Chinese, but our racial stigmata are gray, and our wrists are rusted where once they ran clear. I hate that fellow whose face I see, lost and lonely in my dawn mirror! When I see a fine lady, God! I know outrage. Such spring cartwheel thoughts are not for dead pharaohs. So, with limits, Cal, you can count me in. Good night."

The two phones clicked.

Quartermain leaned out his window. Below, in the moonlight, he could see the pumpkins, shining with a terrible October light.

Why do I imagine, he wondered, *that one is carved to look like me, another one just like*

Bleak, and the other just like Gray? No, no. It can't be. Christ, where do I find Braling's metronome?

"Out of the way!" he yelled into the shadows.

Grabbing his crutches, he struggled to his feet, plunged downstairs, tottered onto the porch, and somehow found his way down to the sidewalk and advanced on the flickering line of Halloween gourds.

"Jesus," he whispered. "Those are the ugliest damned pumpkins I ever saw. So!"

He brandished a crutch and whacked one of the orange ghouls, then another and another until the lights in the pumpkins winked out.

He reared to chop and slash and whack until the gourds were split open, spilling their seeds, orange flesh flung in all directions.

"Someone!" he cried.

His housekeeper, an alarmed expression on her face, burst from the house and raced down the great lawn.

"Is it too late," cried Quartermain, "to light the oven?"

"The oven, Mr. Cal?"

"Light the god-damned oven. Fetch the pie pans. Have you recipes for pumpkin pie?"

"Yes, Mr. Cal."

"Then grab these damn pieces. Tomorrow for lunch: Just Desserts!"

Quartermain turned and crutched himself upstairs.

CHAPTER

Fourteen

THE EMERGENCY MEETING OF THE GREEN TOWN Board of Education was ready to begin.

There were only two there beside Calvin C. Quartermain: Bleak and Miss Flynt, the recording secretary.

He pointed at the pies on the table.

"What's this?" said the other two.

"A victory breakfast, or maybe a lunch."

"It looks like pie to me, Quartermain."

"It *is,* idiot! A victory feast, that's what it is. Miss Flynt?"

"Yes, Mr. Cal?"

"Take a statement. Tonight at sunset, on the edge of the ravine, I will make a few remarks."

"Such as?"

"Rebellious rapscallions, hear this: The war is not done, nor have you lost nor have you won. It seems a draw. Prepare for a long October. I have taken your measure. Beware."

Quartermain paused and shut his eyes, pressed his fingers to his temples, as if trying to remember.

"Oh, yes. Colonel Freeleigh, sorely missed. We need a colonel. How long was Freeleigh a colonel?"

"Since the month Lincoln was shot."

"Well, someone must be a colonel. I'll do that. *Colonel* Quartermain. How does that sound?"

"Pretty fine, Cal, pretty fine."

"All right. Now shut up and eat your pie."

CHAPTER

Fifteen

THE BOYS SAT IN A CIRCLE ON THE PORCH OF Doug and Tom's house. The pale blue painted ceiling mirrored the blue of the October sky.

"Gosh," said Charlie. "I don't like to say it, Doug—but I'm hungry."

"Charlie! You're not thinking right!"

"I'm thinkin' fine," said Charlie. "Strawberry shortcake with a big white summer cloud of whipped cream."

"Tom," said Douglas, "in the by-laws in your nickel tablet, what's it say about treason?"

"Since when is thinking about shortcake treason?" Charlie regarded some wax from his ear with great curiosity.

"It's not thinking, it's *saying*!"

"I'm *starved*," said Charlie. "And the other guys, look, touch 'em and they'd bite. It ain't workin', Doug."

Doug stared around the circle at the faces of his soldiers, as if daring them to add to Charlie's lament.

"In my grandpa's library there's a book that says Hindus starve for ninety days. Don't worry. After the third day you don't feel nothing!"

"How long's it been? Tom, check your watch. How long?"

"Mmmm, one hour and ten minutes."

"Jeez!"

"Whatta you mean 'jeez'? Don't look at your watch! Look at calendars. Seven *days* is a fast!"

They sat a while longer in silence. Then Charlie said, "Tom, how long's it been *now*?"

"Don't tell him, Tom!"

Tom consulted his watch, proudly. "One hour and *twelve* minutes!"

"Holy smoke!" Charlie squeezed his face into

a mask. "My stomach's a *prune*! They'll have to feed me with a tube. I'm dead. Send for my folks. Tell 'em I loved 'em." Charlie shut his eyes and flung himself backward onto the floorboards.

"Two hours," said Tom, later. "Two whole hours we've been starving, Doug. That's sockdolager! If only we can throw up after supper, we're set."

"Boy," said Charlie, "I feel like that time at the dentist and he jammed that needle in me. Numb! And if the other guys had more guts, they'd tell you they're bound for Starved Rock, too. Right, fellas? Think about cheese! How about crackers?"

Everyone moaned.

Charlie ran on. "Chicken à la *king*!"

They groaned.

"Turkey drumsticks!"

"*See*." Tom poked Doug's elbow. "You got 'em writhing! *Now* where's your revolution?!"

"Just one more day!"

"And *then*?"

"Limited rations."

"Gooseberry pie, apple-butter, onion sandwiches?"

"Cut it out, Charlie."

"Grape jam on white *bread*!"

"Stop!"

"No, sir!" Charlie snorted. "Tear off my chevrons, General. This was fun for the first ten minutes. But there's a bulldog in my belly. Gonna go home, sit down real polite, wolf me half a banana cake, two liverwurst sandwiches, and get drummed outta your dumb old army, but at least I'll be a live dog and no shriveled-up mummy, whining for leftovers."

"Charlie," Doug pleaded, "you're our strong right *arm*."

Doug jumped up and made a fist, his face blood-red. All was lost. This was terrible. Right before his face his plan unraveled and the grand revolt was over.

At that very instant the town clock boomed twelve o'clock, noon, the long iron strokes which came as salvation because Doug leapt to the edge of the porch and stared toward the town square, up at that great terrible iron monument, and then down at the grassy park, where all the old men played at their chessboards.

An expression of wild surmise filled Doug's face.

"Hey," he murmured. "Hold on. The chessboards!" he cried. "Starvation's one thing, and that helps, but now I see what our real problem is. Down outside the courthouse, all those terrible old men playing chess."

The boys blinked.

"What?" said Tom.

"Yeah, what?" echoed the boys.

"We're *on* the chessboard!" cried Douglas. "Those chess pieces, those chessmen, those are us! The old guys *move* us on the squares, the streets! All our lives we've been there, trapped on the chessboards in the square, with them shoving us around."

"Doug," said Tom. "You got brains!"

The clock stopped booming. There was a great wondrous silence.

"Well," said Doug, exhaling, "I guess you know what we do *now!*"

CHAPTER

Sixteen

IN THE GREEN PARK BELOW THE MARBLE SHADOW of the courthouse, under the great clock tower's bulk, the chess tables waited.

Now under a gray sky and a faint promise of rain, a dozen chessboards were busy with old men's hands. Above the red and black battlefields, two dozen gray heads were suspended. The pawns and castles and horses and kings and queens trembled and drifted as monarchies fell in ruin.

With the leaf shadows freckling their moves, the old men chewed their insunk mouths and

looked at each other with squints and coldnesses
and sometimes twinkles. They talked in rustles
and scrapings a few feet beyond the monument
to the Civil War dead.

Doug Spaulding snuck up, leaned around the
monument, and watched the moving chess pieces
with apprehension. His chums crept up behind
him. Their eyes lolled over the moving chess pieces
and one by one they moved back and drowsed on
the grass. Doug spied on the old men panting
like dogs over the boards. They twitched. They
twitched again.

Douglas hissed back at his army. "Look!" he
whispered. "That knight's *you,* Charlie! That
king's me!" Doug jerked. "Mr. Weeble's moving
me *now,* ah! Someone *save* me!" He reached out
with stiff arms and froze in place.

The boys' eyes snapped open. They tried to
seize his arms. "We'll help you, Doug!"

"Someone's *moving* me. Mr. Weeble!"

"Darn Weeble!"

At which moment there was a strike of lightning and a following of thunder and a drench of
rain.

"My gosh!" said Doug. "Look."

The rain poured over the courthouse square and the old men jumped up, momentarily forgetting the chess pieces, which tumbled in the deluge.

"Quick, guys, now. Each of you grab as many as you can!" cried Doug.

They all moved forward in a pack, to fall upon the chess pieces.

There was another strike of lightning, another burst of thunder.

"Now!" cried Doug.

There was a third strike of lightning and the boys scrambled, they seized.

The chessboards were empty.

The boys stood laughing at the old men hiding under the trees.

Then, like crazed bats, they rushed off to find shelter.

CHAPTER

Seventeen

"BLEAK!" QUARTERMAIN BARKED INTO HIS telephone.

"Cal?"

"By God, they got the chess pieces that were sent from Italy the year Lincoln was shot. Shrewd damn idiots! Come here tonight. We must plan our counterattack. I'll call Gray."

"Gray's busy dying."

"Christ, he's always dying! We'll have to do it ourselves."

"Steady now, Cal. They're just chess pieces."

"It's what they *signify*, Bleak! This is a full rebellion."

"We'll buy new chess pieces."

"Hell, I might as well be speaking to the dead. Just be here. I'll call Gray and make him put off dying for one more day."

Bleak laughed quietly.

"Why don't we just chuck all those Bolshevik boys into a pot, boil them down to essence of kid?"

"So long, Bleak!"

He rang off and called Gray. The line was busy. He slammed the receiver down, picked it up, and tried again. Listening to the signal, he heard the tapping of tree branches on the window, faintly, far away.

My God, Quartermain thought, *I can hear what he's up to. That's dying all right.*

CHAPTER
Eighteen

THERE WAS THIS OLD HAUNTED HOUSE ON THE far edge of the ravine.

How did they know it was haunted?

Because *they* said so. Everyone knew it.

It had been there for close on to one hundred years and everybody said that while it wasn't haunted during the day, at nighttime strange things happened there.

It seemed a perfectly logical place for the boys to run, Doug leading them and Tom bringing up the rear, carrying their wild treasure, the chess pieces.

It was a grand place to hide because no one—except for a pack of wild boys—would dare come to a haunted house, even if it was full daytime.

The storm still raged and if anyone had looked close at the haunted house, chanced walking through the creaky old doors, down the musty old hallways, up even creakier old stairs, they would have found an attic full of old chairs, smelling of ancient bamboo furniture polish and full of boys with fresh faces who had climbed up in the downfall sounds of the storm, accompanied by intermittent cracks of lightning and thunderclaps of applause, the storm taking delight in its ability to make them climb faster and laugh louder as they leapt and settled, one by one, Indian style, in a circle on the floor.

Douglas pulled a candle stub, lit it, and stuffed it in an old glass candlestick holder. At last, from a burlap gunnysack, he pulled forth and set down, one by one, all the captured chess pieces, naming them for Charlie and Will and Tom and Bo and all the rest. He tossed them forth to settle, like dogs called to war.

"Here's *you,* Charlie." Lightning cracked.

"Yeah!"

"Here's *you*, Willie." Thunder boomed.

"Yeah!"

"And you, Tom."

"That's too small and plain," Tom protested. "Can't I be king?"

"Shut up or you're the queen."

"I'm shut," said Tom.

Douglas finished the list and the boys clustered round, their faces shining with sweat, eager for the next lightning bolt to let loose its electric shower. Distant thunder cleared its throat.

"Listen!" cried Doug. "We've almost got it made. The town's almost ours. We got all the chess pieces, so the old men can't shove us around. Can anyone do better?"

Nobody could and admitted it, happily.

"Just one thing," said Tom. "How'd you work that lightning, Doug?"

"Shut up and listen," said Douglas, aggrieved that central intelligence had almost been wormed away from him.

"The thing is, one way or another, I got the lightning to knock the bellybuttons off the old sailors and Civil War vets on the lawn. They're all home now, dying like flies. Flies."

"Only one thing wrong," said Charlie. "The chess pieces are ours right now, sure. But—I'd give anything for a good hot dog."

"Don't say that!"

At which moment lightning struck a tree right outside the attic window. The boys dropped flat.

"Doug! Heck! Make it stop!"

Eyes shut, Douglas shouted, "I can't! I take it back. I lied!"

Dimly satisfied, the storm went away, grumbling.

As if announcing the arrival of someone or something important, a final distant strike of lightning and a rumble of thunder caused the boys to look toward the stairwell, leading down to the second floor of the house.

Far below, someone cleared his throat.

Douglas pricked his ears, moved to the stairwell, and intuitively called down.

"Grandpa?"

"Seems to be," a voice said from the bottom of the stairs. "You boys are not very good at covering your tracks. You left footprints in the grass all the way across town. I followed along, asking questions along the way, getting directions, and here I am."

Doug swallowed hard and said again: "Grandpa?"

"There seems to be a small commotion back in town," said Grandpa, far below, out of sight.

"Commotion?"

"Something like that," said Grandpa's voice.

"You coming up?"

"No," said Grandpa. "But I have a feeling *you're* coming down. I want you to come see me for a visit and we're gonna have a little talk. And then you've got to run an errand because something has been purloined."

"Purloined?"

"Mr. Poe used that word. If need be, you can go back and check the story and refresh your memory."

"Purloined," said Douglas. "Oh, yeah."

"Whatever was purloined—and right now I'm not quite sure what it was," said Grandpa, far away, "—but whatever it was, I think, son, that it should be returned to where it belongs. There are rumors that the town sheriff has been called, so I think you should hop to it."

Douglas backed off and stared at his companions, who had heard the voice from below and were now frozen, not knowing what to do.

"You got nothing more to say?" called Grandpa from down below. "Well, maybe not here. I'm gonna get going; you know where to find me. I'll expect you there soon."

"Yeah, yes, sir."

Doug and the boys were silent as they listened to Grandpa's footsteps echo throughout the haunted house, along the hall, down the stairs, out onto the porch. And then, nothing.

Douglas turned and Tom held up the burlap sack.

"You need this, Doug?" he whispered.

"Gimme."

Doug grabbed the gunnysack and scraped all the chess pieces up and dropped them, one by one, into the sack. There went Pete and Tom and Bo and all the rest.

Doug shook the gunnysack; it made a dry rattling sound like old men's bones.

And with a last backward glance at his army, Doug started down.

CHAPTER

Nineteen

GRANDPA'S LIBRARY WAS A FINE DARK PLACE bricked with books, so anything could happen there and always did. All you had to do was pull a book from the shelf and open it and suddenly the darkness was not so dark anymore.

Here it was that Grandpa sat in place with now this book and now that in his lap and his gold specs on his nose, welcoming visitors who came to stay for a moment and lingered for an hour.

Even Grandmother paused here, after some burdensome time, as an aging animal seeks the watering place to be refreshed. And Grandfather was always here to offer cups of good clear Walden Pond, or shout down the deep well of Shakespeare and listen, with satisfaction, for echoes.

Here the lion and the hartebeest lay together, here the jackass became unicorn, here on Saturday noon an elderly man could be found underneath a not too imaginary bough, eating bread in the guise of sandwiches and pulling briefly at a jug of cellar wine.

Douglas stood on the edge of it all, waiting.

"Step forward, Douglas," said Grandfather.

Douglas stepped forward, holding the gunnysack in one hand behind his back.

"Got anything to say, Douglas?"

"No, sir."

"Nothing at all about anything?"

"No, sir."

"What you been up to today, son?"

"Nothing."

"A busy nothing or a nothing nothing?"

"A nothing nothing, I guess."

"Douglas." Grandpa paused to polish his gold-rimmed specs. "They say that confession is good for the soul."

"They *do* say that."

"And they must mean it or they wouldn't say it."

"I guess so."

"Know it, Douglas, *know* it. Got anything to confess?"

"About what?" said Douglas, keeping the gunnysack behind him.

"That's what I'm trying to find out. You going to help?"

"Maybe you could give me a hint, sir."

"All right. Seems there was flood tide down at the City Hall courthouse today. I hear a tidal wave of boys inundated the grass. You know *any* of them?"

"No, sir."

"Any of them know *you*?"

"If I don't know them, how could they know me, sir?"

"Is that all you got to say?"

"Right now? Yes, sir."

Grandpa shook his head. "Doug, I told you, I know about the purloineds. And I'm sorry you think you can't tell me about them. But I remember being your age, and getting caught red-handed at doing something I knew I shouldn't do, but I did anyway. Yes, I remember." Grandpa's eyes twinkled behind his specs. "Well, I think I'm holding you up, boy. I think you got somewhere to go."

"Yes, sir."

"Well, try to hurry it up. The rain's still coming down, lightning all over town, and the town square is empty. If you run and let the lightning strike, maybe you'll do a fast job of what you *should* be doing. Does that sound reasonable, Doug?"

"Yes, sir."

"Well then, get to it."

Douglas started to back away.

"Don't back off, son," said Grandpa. "I'm not royalty. Just turn around and skedaddle."

"Skedaddle. Was that originally French, Grampa?"

"Hell." The old man reached for a book. "When you get back, let's look it *up*!"

CHAPTER

Twenty

JUST BEFORE MIDNIGHT, DOUG WOKE TO THAT terrible boredom that only sleep ensures.

It was then, listening to Tom's chuffing breath, deep in an ice-floe summer hibernation, that Doug lifted his arms and wiggled his fingers, like a tuning fork; a gentle vibration ensued. He felt his soul move through an immense timberland.

His feet, shoeless, drifted to the floor and he leaned south to pick up the gentle radio waves of his uncle, down the block. Did he hear the elephant sound of Tantor summoning an ape-boy?

Or, half through the night, had Grandpa, next door, fallen in a grave of slumber, dead to the world, gold specs on his nose, with Edgar Allan Poe shelved to his right and the Civil War dead, truly dead, to his left, waiting in his sleep, it seemed, for Doug to arrive?

So, striking his hands together and wiggling his fingers, Doug made one final vibration of his literary tuning fork and moved with quiet intuition toward his grandparents' house.

Grandpa, in his grave of sleep, whispered a call.

Doug was out the midnight door so fast he almost forgot to catch the screen before it slammed.

Ignoring the elephant trumpet behind, he barefooted into his grandparents' house.

There in the library slept Grandpa, awaiting the breakfast resurrection, open for suggestions.

Now, at midnight, it was the unlit time of the special school, so Doug leaned forward and whispered in Grandpa's ear, "1899."

And Gramps, lost in another time, murmured of that year and how the temperature was and what the people were like moving in that town.

Then Douglas said, "1869."

And Grandpa was lost four years after Lincoln was shot.

Standing there, watching, Douglas realized that if he visited here night after night and spoke to Grandpa, Grandpa, asleep, would be his teacher and that if he spent six months or a year or two years coming to this special long-after-midnight school, he would have an education that nobody else in the world would have. Grandpa would give his knowledge as a teacher, without knowing it, and Doug would drink it in and not tell Tom or his parents or anybody.

"That's it," whispered Doug. "Thank you, Grandpa, for all you say, asleep or awake. And thanks again for today and your advice on the purloineds. I don't want to say any more. I don't want to wake you up."

So Douglas, his ears full up and his mind full brimmed, left his grandpa sleeping there and crept toward the stairs and the tower room because he wanted to have one more encounter with the night town and the moon.

Just then the great clock across town, an immense moon, a full moon of stunned sound and round illumination, cleared its ratchety throat and let free a midnight sound.

One.

Douglas climbed the stairs.

Two. Three.

Four. Five.

Reaching the tower window, Douglas looked out upon an ocean of rooftops and the great monster clock tower as time summed itself up.

Six. Seven.

His heart floundered.

Eight. Nine.

His flesh turned to snow.

Ten. Eleven.

A shower of dark leaves fell from a thousand trees.

Twelve!

Oh my God, yes, he thought.

The clock! Why hadn't he thought of that?

The *clock*!

THE LAST VIBRATION OF THE GREAT CLOCK BELL
faded.

A wind swayed the trees outside and the pekoe
curtain hung out on the air, a pale ghost.

Douglas felt his breath siphon.

You, he thought. *How come I never noticed?*

The great and terrible courthouse clock.

Just last year, hadn't Grandpa laid out the machinery's blueprint, lecturing?

The huge round lunar clock was a gristmill,
he'd said. Shake down all the grains of Time—

the big grains of centuries, and the small grains of years, and the tiny grains of hours and minutes—and the clock pulverized them, slid Time silently out in all directions in a fine pollen, carried by cold winds to blanket the town like dust, everywhere. Spores from that clock lodged in your flesh to wrinkle it, to grow bones to monstrous size, to burst feet from shoes like turnips. Oh, how that great machine at the town's center dispensed Time in blowing weathers.

The clock!

That was the thing that bleached and ruined life, jerked people out of bed, hounded them to schools and graves! Not Quartermain and his band of old men, or Braling and his metronome; it was the clock that ran this town like a church.

Even on the clearest of nights it was misted, glowing, luminous, and old. It rose above town like a great dark burial mound, drawn to the skies by the summoning of the moon, calling out in a grieved voice of days long gone, and days that would come no more, whispering of other autumns when the town was young and all was beginning and there was no end.

"So it's you," whispered Douglas.

Midnight, said the clock. *Time,* it said, *Darkness.* Flights of night birds flew up to carry the final peal away, out over the lake and into the night country, gone.

Doug yanked down the shade so Time could not blow through the screen.

The clock light shone on the sidings of the house like a mist breathing on the windows.

CHAPTER

Twenty-Two

"BOY, I JUST HEARD THE CRAZIEST THINGS."
Charlie strolled up, chewing on a clover-blossom.
"I got me a secret service report from some girls."

"Girls!"

Charlie smiled at how his ten-inch firecracker
had blown the laziness off his pals' faces. "My
sister said way back last July they got old lady
Bentley to admit she never *was* young. I thought
you'd like *that* news."

"Charlie, *Charlie*!"

"Burden of proof," said Charlie. "The girls told

me that old lady Bentley showed some pictures, junk and stuff, which didn't prove nothin'. Fact is, when you think on it, fellas, none of these old ginks look like they were *ever* young."

"Why didn't *you* think of that, Doug?" said Tom.

"Why don't *you* shut up?" said Douglas.

"I guess this makes me a lieutenant," said Charlie.

"You just moved up to sergeant *yesterday*!"

Charlie stared hard at Douglas for a long moment.

"Okay, okay, you're a lieutenant," said Douglas.

"Thanks," said Charlie. "What'll we do about my sister? She wants to be part of our army—a special spy."

"To heck with her!"

"You got to admit that's great secret stuff she turned in."

"Boy, Charlie, you sure *think* of things," said Tom. "Doug, why don't *you* think of things?"

"Darn it!" cried Douglas. "Whose idea was the graveyard tour, the candy, the food, the chess pieces, all *that*?"

"Hold on," said Tom. "The graveyard tour, I said that. The candy, yeah, was yours, but I gotta tell ya, the food experiment was a failure. Heck, you haven't said anything new in a coupla hours. And all the chessboards are full of chess pieces again and those old men are busy pushing the pieces—us—around. Any moment now we'll feel ourselves grabbed and moved and we won't be able to live our own lives anymore."

Douglas could feel Charlie and Tom creeping up on him, taking the war out of his hands like a ripe plum. Private, corporal, sergeant, lieutenant. Today, lieutenant; tomorrow captain. And the day after?

"It's not just ideas that count." Douglas wiped his brow. "It's how you stick 'em together. Take this fact of Charlie's—it's secondhand. Heck, *girls* thought of it *first*!"

Everybody's eyebrows went up.

Charlie's face fell.

"And anyway," Douglas went on, "I'm puttin' ideas together for a real bang-up revelation."

They all looked at him, waiting.

"Okay, Doug, go on," said Charlie.

Douglas shut his eyes. "And the revelation is:

Since old people don't *look* like they were ever kids, they never *were*! So they're not humans at *all*!"

"What *are* they, Doug?"

"Another *race*!"

Everybody sat, stunned by the vast sunburst caused by this explosion, this incredible revelation. It rained upon them in fire and flames.

"Yes, another race," said Douglas. "Aliens. Evil. And we, we're the slaves they keep for nefarious odd jobs and punishments!"

Everybody melted with the after-effects of this announcement.

Charlie stood up solemnly and announced: "Doug, old pal, see this beanie on my head? I'm taking my beanie *off* to *you*!" Charlie raised his beanie to applause and laughter.

They all smiled at Doug, their general, their leader, who took out his pocketknife and casually started a philosophical game of one-finger mumblety-peg.

"Yeah, but . . ." said Tom, and went on. "The last thing you said didn't work out. It's okay to *say* the old people are from another planet, but what about Grandpa and Grandma? We've known them all our lives. Are you saying that they're aliens, too?"

Doug's face turned red. He hadn't quite worked this part out, and here was his brother—his second-in-command, his junior officer—questioning his theory.

"And," Tom went on, "what do we have new in the way of *action,* Doug? We can't just sit here. What do we do next?"

Doug swallowed hard. Before he had a chance to speak, Tom, now that everybody was looking at him, said slowly, "The only thing that comes to mind right now is maybe we stop the courthouse clock. You can hear that darned thing ticking all over town. Bong! Midnight! Whang! Get outta bed! Boom! Jump into bed! Up down, up down, over and over."

Ohmigosh, thought Douglas. *I saw it last night. The clock! Why in heck didn't I say so first?*

Tom picked his nose calmly. "Why don't we just lambaste that darn old clock—kill it dead! Then we can do *whatever* we want to do *whenever* we want to do it. Okay?"

Everyone stared at Tom. Then they began to

cheer and yell, even Douglas, trying to forget it was his younger brother, not himself, who was saving the day.

"Tom!" they all shouted. "Good old Tom!"

"Ain't nothin'," said Tom. He looked to his brother. "When do we kill the blasted thing?"

Douglas bleated, his tongue frozen. The soldiers stared, waiting.

"Tonight?" said Tom.

"*I* was just going to say that!" Douglas cried.

CHAPTER

Twenty-Three

THE COURTHOUSE CLOCK SOMEHOW KNEW THEY were coming to kill it.

It loomed high above the town square with its great marble façade and sun-blazed face, a frozen avalanche, waiting to bury the assassins. Simultaneously, it allowed the leaders of its religion and philosophy, the ancient gray-haired messengers of Time and dissolution, to pass through the thundering bronze doors below.

Douglas, watching the soldiery of death and mummification slip calmly through the dark portals, felt a stir of panic. There, in the shellac-smelling, paper-rustling rooms of Town Hall, the Board of Education slyly unmade destinies, pared calendars, devoured Saturdays in torrents of homework, instigated reprimands, tortures, and criminalities. Their dead hands pulled streets straighter, loosed rivers of asphalt over soft dirt to make roads harder, more confining, so that open country and freedom were pushed further and further away, so that one day, years from now, green hills would be a distant echo, so far off that it would take a lifetime of travel to reach the edge of the city and peer out at one lone small forest of dying trees.

Here in this one building, lives were slotted, alphabetized in files and fingerprints; the children's destinies put under seal! Men with blizzard faces and lightning-colored hair, carrying Time in their briefcases, hurried by to serve the clock, to run it with great sprockets and gears. At twilight they stepped out, all smiles, having found new ways to constrict, imprison, or entangle lives in fees and licenses. You could not even prove your death without these men, this building, this clock, and a certificate duly inked, stamped, and signed.

"Here we are," whispered Douglas, all his pals clustered around him. "It's almost quittin' time. We gotta be careful. If we wait too long it'll be so shut up there'll be no way to get in. Right at twilight, when the last doors are being locked, that's when we make our move, right? As they come out, we go in."

"Right," said everyone.

"So," said Douglas. "Hold your breath."

"It's held," said Tom. "But Doug, I got something to say."

"What?" said Doug.

"You know that no matter when we go in, if we go in all together, someone's going to see us and they're going to remember our faces and we're going to get in trouble. It was bad enough with the chess pieces out front of the courthouse. We were seen, and we had to give everything back. So, why don't we wait until it's all locked up?"

"We can't do that. I just said why."

"Tell you what," said Tom. "Why don't I go in now and hide in the men's until everyone's gone home? Then I'll sneak upstairs and let you in one of the windows near the clock tower. Up there, on the third floor." He pointed to a spot high up the ancient brick walls.

"Hey!" said all the gang.

"That won't work," said Doug.

"Why not?" said Tom.

Before Doug had time to think of a reason, Charlie piped up.

"Sure it'll work," said Charlie. "Tom's right. Tom, you want to go in and hide now?"

"Sure," said Tom.

Everyone was looking at Doug, still their general, and he had to give his approval.

"What I don't like," said Doug, "is smart alecks who think they know everything. Okay, go in and hide. When it gets dark, let us in."

"Okay," said Tom.

And he was gone.

People were coming out through the big bronze doors and Doug and the others pulled back around the corner of the building and waited for the sun to go down.

CHAPTER

Twenty-Four

THE COURTHOUSE WAS FINALLY COMPLETELY quiet and the night was dark and the boys climbed up the fire escape on the side of the building, very quietly, until they got up to the third floor, near the clock tower.

They stopped at the window where Tom was supposed to appear, but no one was there.

"Gosh," said Doug. "I hope he didn't get locked in the men's room."

"They never lock the men's room," said Charlie. "He'll be here."

And sure enough, all of a sudden, there was Tom behind the glass pane, waving to them and opening and shutting his mouth, but they couldn't hear what he was saying.

At long last he raised the window and the smell of the courthouse rushed out into the night around them.

"Get in," commanded Tom.

"We are," said Doug, angrily.

One by one the boys crawled inside the courthouse and snuck along the hallways till they reached the clock machinery door.

"I bet you," said Tom, "this darned door's locked, too."

"No bets," said Doug, and rattled the doorknob. "Good grief! Tom, I hate to say it, but you're right. Has anybody got a firecracker?"

Suddenly six hands reached into six dungaree pockets and just as suddenly reappeared with three four-inchers and a few five-inch crackers.

"It's no good," said Tom, "unless someone has matches."

More hands reached out with matches in each.

Doug stared at the door.

"How can we fix the crackers so they'll really do some good when they go off?"

"Glue," said Tom.

Doug shook his head, scowling.

"Yeah, glue, right," he said. "Does anyone just happen to have any *glue* on them?"

A single hand reached out on the air. It was Pete's.

"Here's some Bulldog glue," he said. "Bought it for my airplane models and because I like the great picture of the bulldog on the label."

"Let's give it a try."

Doug applied glue along the length of one of the five-inchers and pressed it against the outside of the machinery room door.

"Stand back," he said, and struck a match.

With his mob back in the shadows and his hands over his ears, Doug waited for the cracker to go off. The orange flame sizzled and zipped along the fuse.

There was a beautiful explosion.

For a long moment they all stared at the door in disappointment and then, very slowly, it drifted open.

"I was right," said Tom.

"Why don't you just shut up," said Doug. "C'mon."

He pulled the door and it opened wide.

There was a sound below.

"Who's there?" a voice cried from deep down in the courthouse.

"Ohmigosh," whispered Tom. "I bet that's the janitor."

"Who's up there?" the voice cried again.

"Quick!" said Doug, leading his army through the door.

And now, at last, they were inside the clock.

Here, suddenly, was the immense, frightening machinery of the Enemy, the Teller of Lives and Time. Here was the core of the town and its existence. Doug could feel all of the lives of the people he knew moving in the clock, suspended in bright oils and meshed in sharp cogs and ground down in clamped springs that clicked onward with no stopping. The clock moved silently. And now he knew that it had *never* ticked. No one in the town had ever actually heard it counting to itself; they had only listened so hard that they had heard their own hearts and the time of their lives moving in their wrists and their hearts and their heads. For here was only cold metal silence, quiet motion, gleams and glitters, murmurs and faint whispers of steel and brass.

Douglas trembled.

They were together at last, Doug and the clock that had risen like a lunar face throughout his life at every midnight. At any moment the great machine might uncoil its brass springs, snatch him up, and dump him in a grinder of cogs to mesh its endless future with his blood, in a forest of teeth and tines, waiting, like a music box, to play and tune his body, ribboning his flesh.

And then, as if it had waited just for this moment, the clock cleared its throat with a sound like July thunder. The vast spring hunched in upon itself as a cannon prepares for its next concussion. Before Douglas could turn, the clock erupted.

One! Two! Three!

It fired its bells! And he was a moth, a mouse in a bucket being kicked, and kicked again. An earthquake shook the tower, jolting him off his feet.

Four! Five! Six!

He staggered, clapping his hands over his ears to keep them from bursting.

Again, again—*Seven! Eight!*—the tempest tore the air. Shaken he fell against the wall, eyes shut, his heart stopped with each storm of sound.

"Quick!" Douglas shouted. "The crackers!"

"Kill the darn thing!" shouted Tom.

"I'm supposed to say that," said Doug. "Kill it!"

There was a striking of matches and a lighting of fuses and the crackers were thrown into the maw of the vast machine.

Then there was a wild stomping and commotion as the boys fled.

They bolted through the third-floor window and almost fell down the fire escape and as they reached the bottom great explosions burst from the courthouse tower; a great metal racketing clangor. The clock struck again and again, over and over as it fought for its life. Pigeons blew like torn papers tossed from the roof. *Bong!* The clock voice chopped concussions to split the heavens. Ricochets, grindings, a last desperate twitch of hands. Then . . .

Silence.

At the bottom of the fire escape all the boys gazed up at the dead machine. There was no ticking, imagined or otherwise, no singing of birds, no purr of motors, only the soft exhalations of sleeping houses.

At any moment the boys, looking up, expected the slain tower face, hands, numerals, guts, to groan, slide, and tumble in a grinding avalanche of brass intestines and iron meteor showers, down, down upon the lawn, heaping, rumbling, burying them in minutes, hours, years, and eternities.

But there was only silence and the clock, a mindless ghost, hanging in the sky with limp, dead hands, saying naught, doing nothing. Silence and yet another long silence, while all about lights blinked on in houses, bright winks stretching out into the country, and people began to come out on porches and wonder at the darkening sky.

Douglas stared up, all drenched with sweat, and was about to speak when:

"I *did* it!" cried Tom.

"Tom!" cried Doug. "*We!* All of us did it. But, good grief, what did we do?"

"Before it falls on us," said Tom, "we'd better run."

"Who says?" said Douglas.

"Sorry," said Tom.

"Run!" cried Doug.

And the victorious army ran away into the night.

CHAPTER

Twenty-Five

IT WAS THE MIDDLE OF THE NIGHT AND TOM still couldn't sleep.

Doug knew this because several times he heard Tom's bedclothes fall to the floor, as if he were tossing and turning, and each time he heard the sound of the sheets and coverlet being reassembled.

At about two in the morning Doug went down to the icebox and brought a dish of ice cream up to Tom, which, he figured, might cause Tom to speak more freely.

Tom sat up in bed and hardly touched the ice cream. He sat there staring at it as it melted and then said, "Doug, an awful thing has happened."

"Yeah, Tom," said Doug.

"We thought if we stopped the big courthouse clock we might stop the old people from holding on to—stealing—our time. But nothing's been stopped, has it?"

"No, sir," said Doug.

"I mean," said Tom, "Time's still moving. Nothing's changed. Running home, I looked at all the lights around us and none of them had gone out. I saw some policemen in the distance, down the street, and they hadn't been stopped. I kept waiting for all the lights to go out or something to happen to show that we'd really *done* something. But instead it looks as if someone might have been hurt. I mean, when you think about Will and Bo and the others, kinda limping home from the courthouse. I've got a feeling nobody's gonna sleep tonight and maybe when they do get to sleep, they'll sleep late, my gosh, they're gonna lie around, doing nothin', staying in bed, keeping quiet, and here I am for the first time in years, wide awake. I can't even shut my eyes. What are we going to do about it, Doug? I mean, you kept saying we had to kill the clock, but how do we make it live again, if we have to?"

"The clock wasn't alive," said Doug softly.

"But you said," said Tom. "Well, *I* said. I guess I started it. We all kept saying that we had to do it in, so we did, but what now? It looks like we'll all be in trouble now," Tom finished.

"Only me," said Doug. "Grandpa will give me a talking-to."

"But we went along, Doug. It was swell. We liked it. We had *fun*. But now, if the clock was never alive, how do we bring it back from the dead? We can't have it both ways, but something's got to be done. What's next?"

"Maybe I've got to go down to the courthouse and sign some sort of paper," said Doug. "I could tell 'em I'll give them my allowance for eight or ten years, so they can fix that clock."

"Ohmigosh, Doug!"

"That's about the size of it," said Doug, "when you want to revive a big thing like that. Eight or ten years. But what the heck, I guess I deserve it.

So maybe tomorrow I'll go down and turn my-self in."

"I'll go with you, Doug."

"No, sir," said Doug.

"Yes, I will. You're not going anywhere with-out old Tom."

"Tom," said Doug. "I got only one thing to say to you."

"What?"

"I'm glad I've got you for a younger brother."

Doug turned, his face flushed, and started to walk out of the room.

"I think I can make you gladder," said Tom.

Doug halted.

"When you think about the money," said Tom. "What if the whole gang of us, the whole mob, went up in the clock tower and cleaned it up, if we did the whole machine over somehow? We couldn't repair the whole darned thing, no, but we could spend a couple hours and make it look right and maybe run right, maybe we could save all the expenses and save *you* from being a slave for the rest of your life."

"I don't know," said Doug.

"We could give it a try," said Tom. "Ask

Grandpa. He'll ask the courthouse people if they'll let us up there again, this time with lots of polish and oil and sweat, and maybe we could bring the darn dead machine back to life. It's gotta work. It's *gonna* work, Doug. Let's do it."

Doug turned and walked back to Tom's bed and sat on the edge. "Dibs on some of that ice cream," he said.

"Sure," said Tom. "You get the first bite."

CHAPTER

Twenty-Six

THE NEXT DAY, AT NOON, DOUGLAS WALKED home from school to have lunch. When he got there, his mother sent him straight next door to his grandparents' house. Grandpa was waiting, sitting in his favorite chair in a pool of light from his favorite lamp, in the library, where all was stillness and all the books on the shelves were standing alert and ready to be read.

Hearing the front door open, Grandpa, without looking up from his book, said, "Douglas?"

"Yeah."

"Come in, boy, and sit down."

It wasn't often that Grandpa offered you a chance to sit down, which meant there was very serious business ahead.

Douglas entered quietly and sat on the sofa across from Grandpa and waited.

Finally Grandpa put aside his book, which was also a sign of the serious nature of things, and took off his gold-rimmed specs, which was even more serious, and looked at Douglas with what could only be called a piercing stare.

"Now, Doug," he said, "I've been reading one of my favorite authors, Mr. Conan Doyle, and one of my favorite characters in all the books by Conan Doyle is Mr. Sherlock Holmes. He has honed my spirit and sharpened my aspects. So on a day like today, I woke up feeling very much like that detective on Baker Street in London a long time ago."

"Yes, sir," said Douglas, quietly.

"I've been putting together bits and pieces of information and it seems to me that right now the town is afflicted by lots of boys who are suddenly staying home from school, sick, they say, or something or other. Number one is this: I heard tell from Grandma this morning a full report from your house next door. It seems that your brother Tom is doing poorly."

"I wouldn't say that exactly," said Doug.

"Well, if you won't, I will," said Grandpa. "He feels poorly enough to stay home from school. It's not often Tom feels poorly. He's usually so full of pep and energy, I rarely see him when he isn't running. You have any idea about his affliction, Doug?"

"No, sir," said Doug.

"I would hate to contradict you, boy, but I think you do know. But wait for me to add up all the other clues. I got a list here of the boys in your group, the ones I regularly see running under the apple trees, or climbing in them, or kicking the can down the street. They're usually the ones with firecrackers in one hand and a lit match in the other."

At this Douglas shut his eyes and swallowed hard.

"I made it my business," said Grandpa, "to call the homes of all those boys and, strange to say, they're all in bed. That seems most peculiar, Doug. Can you give me any reason why? Those boys are usually like squirrels on the sidewalk, you can't see 'em they move so fast. But they're all feeling sick, sleeping late. How about you, Doug?"

"I'm fine."

"Really?"

"Yes, sir."

"You don't look so fine to me. In fact, you look a little bit under the weather. Taking that together with the boys missing school and Tom feeling poorly and here you are, looking kind of pale around the gills, I figure there must have been some great commotion somewhere last night."

Grandpa stopped and picked up a piece of paper he'd been holding on his lap.

"I got a phone call a little earlier from the courthouse clerk. It seems they found a whole lot of firecracker paper somewhere in the City Hall this morning. Now that is a most peculiar place to find burnt firecracker paper. The clerk told me they're going to have to do quite a lot of repairs in City Hall. They don't say quite what it is they have to fix, but the bill is sizeable and I figure if we apportion it out to various homesteads in the town, it will come to about . . ." Here Grandpa put his glasses back on his fine big nose before continuing. ". . . $70.90 per homestead. Now, most of the people I know around here don't have that kind of money. In order to get it, the people in those homes will have to work quite a few days or maybe weeks or, who knows, months. Would you like to see the list of repairs that have to be done in City Hall, Doug? I've got it right here."

"I don't think so," said Doug.

"I think you'd better look and study, boy. Here goes." He handed the piece of paper to Doug.

Doug stared at the list. His eyes were so fogged that he couldn't read it. The numbers were immense and they seemed to extend far into the future, not just weeks or months, but ohmigosh, years.

"Doug, I want you to do me a favor," said Grandpa. "I want you to take this list and play the part of doctor. I want you to make a series of house calls when school lets out for the day. First of all, go over to your house and see how Tom is doing. Tell him that Grandpa wants him to buy a couple of Eskimo Pies and come over and eat them on the front porch with me this afternoon.

Say that to Tom, Doug, and see if his face doesn't brighten up."

"Yes, sir," said Doug.

"Then, later, I want you to go to all the other boys' houses and see how your friends are doing. Afterward, come back and give me a report, because all those boys who are lying low need something to make them sit up in bed. I'll be waiting for you. Does that seem fair to you?"

"Yes, sir," said Doug, and stood up. "Grandpa, can I say something?"

"What's that, Doug?"

"You're pretty great, Grandpa."

Grandpa mused over that for a few moments before saying, "Not great, Doug, just perceptive. Have you ever looked that word up in Webster's Dictionary?"

"No, sir."

"Well, before you leave, open Mr. Webster and see what he has to say."

CHAPTER

Twenty-Seven

IT WAS GETTING LATE AND THEY WERE STILL UP in the clock tower, nine boys working and cleaning out the firecracker dust and bits of burnt paper. It made a neat little pile outside the door.

It was a hot evening and all the boys were perspiring and talking under their breath and wishing they were somewhere else, almost wishing they were in school, which would be better than this.

When Doug looked out the clock tower window, he could see Grandpa standing down below, looking up, very quietly.

When Grandpa saw Doug looking down, he nodded at him and gave him the merest wave with the stub of his cigar.

Finally the last twilight was gone and full darkness descended and the janitor came in. There was lubricant to be put on the big cog and wheels of the clock. The boys watched with a mixture of fascination and fear. Here was their nemesis, which they thought they'd defeated, being brought back to life. And, they'd helped. In the weak light from a naked ceiling bulb they watched as the janitor wound up the great spring and stood back. There was a rasping shudder from deep within the great clock's innards, and as if afflicted, the boys moved away, shivering.

The big clock began to tick and the boys knew it wouldn't be long till the hour would strike, so they backed off and fled out the door, down the stairs, with Doug following and Tom leading the way.

The mob met Grandpa in the middle of the courthouse lawn and he gave each of them a pat on the head or the shoulder. Then the other boys ran to their homes, leaving Tom and Doug and Grandpa to walk a block to the corner where the

United Cigar Store still stood open because it was Saturday night.

The last of the Saturday night strollers were starting to drift home and Grandpa picked out the finest cigar he could find, cut it, and lit it from the eternal flame that stood on the cigar store counter. He puffed contentedly and looked with quiet satisfaction upon his two grandsons.

"Well done, boys," he said. "Well done."

Then the sound that they didn't want to hear came.

The great clock was clearing its throat in the tower and struck its first note.

Bong!

One by one the town lights began to go out.

Bong!

Grandpa turned and nodded, and gestured with his cigar for the boys to follow him home.

They crossed the street and walked up the block as the great clock struck another note, and another, which shivered the air and trembled their blood.

The boys grew pale.

Grandpa looked down and pretended not to notice.

All the town's lights were now out and they had to find their way in the dark, with only the merest sliver of moon in the sky to lead the way.

They walked away from the clock and its terrible sound, which echoed in their blood and compelled all the people in the town toward their destinies.

They went down past the ravine where, maybe, a new Lonely One was hiding and might come up at any moment and grab hold.

Doug looked out and saw the black silhouette of the haunted house, perched on the edge of the ravine, and wondered.

Then, at last, in the total dark, as the last peal of the great clock faded away, they ambled up the sidewalk and Grandpa said, "Sleep well, boys. God bless."

The boys ran home to their beds. They could feel, though they did not hear, the great clock ticking and the future rushing upon them in the black night.

In the dark Doug heard Tom say from his room across the hall, "Doug?"

"What?"

"That wasn't so hard after all."

"No," said Doug. "Not so hard."

"We did it. At least we put things back the way they should be."

"I don't know about that," said Doug.

"But I know," said Tom, "because that darned clock is going to make the sun rise. I can hardly wait."

Then Tom was asleep and Doug soon followed.

CHAPTER

Twenty-Eight

BONG!

Calvin C. Quartermain stirred in his sleep and slowly rose to an upright position.

Bong!

The great clock, striking midnight.

He felt himself, half-crippled, making it to the window and opening it wide to the sound of the great clock.

Bong!

"It can't be," he murmured to himself. "Not dead. *Not* dead. They fixed the damned thing.

Call the others first thing in the morning. Maybe it's over. Maybe it's done. Anyway, the town's running again the way it's supposed to, and tomorrow I have to figure out what to do next."

He reached up and found an odd thing on his mouth. A smile. He put his hand up to catch it, and, if possible, examine it.

Could be the weather, he thought. *Could be the wind, it's just right. Or maybe I had some sort of twisted dream—what was I dreaming?—and now that the clock is alive again . . . I've got to figure it out. The war is almost over. But how do I finish it? And how do I win?*

Quartermain leaned out the window and gazed at the moon, a silver sliver in the midnight sky. The moon, the clock, his creaking bones. Quartermain recalled numberless nights spent looking out the window at the sleeping town, although in years past his back was not stooped, his joints not stiff; in years past, looking out this very window, he was young, fit as a fiddle, full of piss and vinegar, just like those boys . . .

Wait a minute! Whose birthday's next? he wondered, trying to call up school record sheets in his mind. One of the monsters? What a chance that would be. I'll kill them with kindness, change my spots, dress in a dog suit, hide the mean cat inside!

They won't know what hit them.

CHAPTER

Twenty-Nine

IT WAS SUCH A DAY THAT ALL THE DOORS STOOD open and all the window sashes had been up since dawn. No one could stay in, everyone was out, nobody would die, everyone would live forever. It was more spring than farewell summer, more Eden than Illinois. During the night a rain had come to quench the heat, and in the morning, with the clouds hastened off, each tree in all the yards gave off a separate and private rain if you shook it in passing.

Quartermain, out of bed and whirring through

the house in hand-propelled trajectories, again found that odd thing, a smile, on his mouth.

He kicked the kitchen door wide and flung himself, eyes glittering, the smile pinned to his thin lips, into the presence of his servants and—

The cake.

"Good morning, Mr. Cal," said the cook.

The cake stood like a magnificent Alp upon the kitchen table. To the odors of morning were added the smells of snow upon a white mountain, the aroma of frosted blossoms and candied roses, of petal pink candles and translucent icing. There it was, like a distant hill in a dream of the future, the cake as white as noon clouds, the cake in the shape of collected years, each candle ready for the lighting and blowing out.

"That," he whispered, "oh, my God, that will *do* it! Take it down to the ravine. Get."

The housekeeper and the gardener picked up the white mountain. The cook led the way, opening the door.

They carried it out the door and down the porch and across the garden.

Who could resist a sweet thing like that, a dream? thought Quartermain.

"Watch it!"

The housekeeper slipped on the dew-wet grass.

Quartermain shut his eyes.

"No, God, no!"

When he opened his eyes again, the servants were still marching steadily, perspiring, down the hill, into the green ravine, toward the clear waters, under the high cool shadowy trees, toward the birthday table.

"Thank you," murmured Quartermain, and added, "God."

Below, in the ravine, the cake was set upon the table, and it was white and it glowed and it was perfect.

CHAPTER
Thirty

"THERE," SAID MOTHER, FIXING HIS TIE.

"Who cares about a darn girl's birthday party?" said Douglas. "It sounds awful."

"If Quartermain can go to all the trouble to have a cake made for Lisabell, you can take an hour and go. Especially since he sent invitations. Be polite is all I ask."

"Come on, Doug, aw come on!" cried Tom, from the front porch.

"Hold your horses! Here I go."

And the screen door slammed and he was in

the street and he and Tom were walking in the fresh day.

"Boy," whispered Tom, smiling, "I'm gonna eat till I get sick."

"There's a deep and dire plot in here somewhere," said Douglas. "How come all of a sudden Quartermain isn't making a commotion? How come, just like that, he's all smiles?"

"I never in my life," said Tom, "argued with a piece of cake or a bowl of ice cream."

Halfway down the block they were joined by Charlie, who fell into step beside them and looked like he was going to a funeral.

"Hey, this tie's killing me." Charlie walked with them in a solemn line.

Moments later they were joined by Will and the others.

"As soon as the party's over, let's all go skinny-dipping out at Apple Crick. Might be our last chance before it gets too cold. Summer's gone."

Doug said, "Am I the only one who thinks there's somethin' fishy goin' on here? I mean, why's old man Quartermain giving Lisabell a birthday party? Why'd he invite *us*? I smell a rat, fellas."

Charlie tugged at his tie and said, "I hate to say this, Doug, but it looks like any day now, whatever's left of our war ain't going to be nothing. There doesn't seem to be any *reason* to fight them anymore."

"I don't know, Charlie. Something just doesn't add up."

They came to the ravine and stopped.

"Well, here we are," said Douglas. "Keep your eyes peeled. If I give the word, break and scatter. You fellas go ahead," said Douglas. "I'll be down in a minute. I've got some strategizing to do."

Reluctantly they left him and started down the hill. After they had gone a hundred feet they began to shuffle and then lope, and then run, yelling. They pulled up below, by the tables, and from a distance, here and there through the ravine, like white birds skimming the grass, came the girls, running too, all gathered in one place, and there was Calvin C. Quartermain, reeling down the pathway in a wheelchair, calling out in a high and cheerful voice.

"Hell," said Douglas, standing back alone. "I mean, heck."

The children gathered, shoving and pushing

and laughing. Seen from a distance they were like little figures on a beautiful stage. Their laughter came drifting up to Douglas and his mouth twitched.

And then, beyond the children, resplendent on its own white-clothed table, was the birthday cake. Douglas stared.

It rose, tier upon tier, of such a size that it towered like a snowman, magnificent and shining in the sun.

"Doug, hey, Doug!" voices drifted up to him.

But he didn't hear.

The cake, the white and beautiful cake, a piece of winter saved from years ago, cool and snowy now in the late summer day. The cake, the white and magnificent cake, frost and rime and snow-flakes, apple-flower and lily-bud. And the voices laughing and the laughter rolling up to him where he stood alone and separate and their voices calling, "Doug, come on, aw, Doug, come down. Hey, Doug, aw come on . . ."

His eyes were blinded by the frost and the snow of it. He felt his feet propelling him down into the ravine and he knew he was moving toward the table and the white vision, and there was no way to stop his feet, no way to turn his eyes away, and all thoughts of battle plans and troop movements fled from his mind. He began to shuffle and he began to lope and then he ran faster and faster, and reaching a large tree, he grabbed hold to catch his breath. He heard himself whisper, "Hi."

And everyone, looking at him, in the light of the snow mountain, in the glare of the wintry hill, replied, "Hi." And he joined the party.

There was Lisabell. Among the others she stood, her face as delicate as the curlicues on the frosted cake, her lips soft and pink as the birthday candles. Her great eyes fixed him where he stood. He was suddenly conscious of the grass under his shoes. His throat was dry. His tongue filled his mouth. The children milled round and round, with Lisabell at the center of their carousel.

Quartermain came hurtling along the rough path, his wheelchair almost flying, and nearly crashed into the table. He gave a cry and sat on the outer edge of the milling crowd, a look of immense satisfaction on his creased yellow face.

And then Mr. Bleak appeared and stood behind

the wheelchair, smiling an altogether different kind of smile.

Douglas watched as Lisabell bent toward the cake. The soft scent of the candles wafted on the breeze. And there was her face, like a summer peach, beautiful and warm, and the light of the candles reflected in her dark eyes. Douglas held his breath. The entire world waited and held its breath. Quartermain was frozen, gripping his chair as if it were his own body threatening to run off with him. Fourteen candles. Fourteen years to be snuffed out and a goal set toward one more as good or better. Lisabell seemed happy. She was floating down the great river of Time and enjoying the trip, blissful with her journeying. The happiness of the insane was in her eye and hand.

She exhaled a great breath, the smell of a summer apple.

The candles snuffed out.

The boys and girls crowded to the cake as Lisabell picked up a great silver knife. The sun glinted off its edge in flashes that seared the eyes. She cut the cake and pushed the slice with the knife and slipped it onto a plate. This plate she picked up and held with two hands. The cake was white and soft and sweet-looking. Everyone stared at it. Old man Quartermain grinned like an idiot. Bleak smiled sadly.

"Who shall I give the first piece to?" Lisabell cried.

She deliberated so long it seemed she must be putting a part of herself into the soft color and spun sugar of the frosting.

She took two slow steps forward. She was not smiling now. Her face was gravely serious. She held out the cake upon the plate and handed it to Douglas.

She stood before Doug and moved her face so close to his that he could feel her breath on his cheeks.

Douglas, startled, jumped back.

Shocked, Lisabell opened her eyes as she cried softly a word he could not at first hear.

"Coward," she cried. "And not only that," she added. "Scaredy-cat!"

"Don't listen, Doug," said Tom.

"Yeah, you don't have to take that," said Charlie.

Douglas moved back another step, blinking.

Douglas held the plate in his hands and the children stood around him. He did not see Quartermain wink at Bleak and jab him with his elbow. He saw only Lisabell's face. It was a face with snow in it, with cherries, and water and grass, and it was a face like this late afternoon. It was a face that looked into him. He felt as if, somehow, she had touched him, here, there, upon the eyelids, the ears, the nose. He shivered. He took a bite of cake.

"Well," said Lisabell. "Got nothing to say? If you're scared down here, I bet you're even more scared up there." She pointed upward, toward the far edge of the ravine. "Tonight," she said, "we're all going to be there. I bet you won't even show up."

Doug looked from her up to the top of the ravine and there stood the haunted house where, in the daytime, the boys sometimes gathered, but where they never dared to go at night.

"Well," said Lisabell. "What are you waiting for? Will you be there or not?"

"Doug," said Tom. "You don't have to take that. Give her what for, Doug."

Doug looked from Lisabell's face up to the

heights of the ravine and again to the haunted house.

The cake melted in Douglas's mouth. Between looking at the house and trying to decide, with the cake in his mouth, sugar melting on his tongue, he didn't know what to do. His heart was beating wildly and his face was a confusion of blood.

"I'll . . ." he blurted.

"You'll what?" taunted Lisabell.

". . . be there," he said.

"Thatta boy, Doug," said Tom.

"Don't let her fool you," said Bo.

But Doug turned away from his friends.

Suddenly a memory came to him. Years ago, he had killed a butterfly on a bush, smashing it with a stick, for no reason at all, other than it seemed like the thing to do. Glancing up, he had seen his grandfather, like a framed picture, startled, on the porch above him. Douglas dropped the stick and picked up the shattered flakes of butterfly, the bright pieces of sun and grass. He tried to fit it back together again and breathe a spell of life into it. But at last, crying, he said, "I'm sorry."

And then Grandpa had spoken, saying, "Remember, always, everything moves." Thinking of the butterfly, he was reminded of Quartermain. The trees shook with wind and suddenly he was looking out of Quartermain's face, and he knew how it felt to be inside a haunted house, alone. He went to the birthday table and picked up a plate with the largest piece of cake on it, and began to walk toward Quartermain. There was a starched look in the old man's face, then a searching of the boy's eyes and chin and nose with a sunless gaze.

Douglas stopped before the wheelchair.

"Mr. Quartermain," he said.

He pushed the plate out on the warm air into Quartermain's hands.

At first the old man's hands did not move. Then as if wakened, his fingers opened with surprise. Quartermain regarded the gift with utter bewilderment.

"Thank you," he said, so low no one heard him. He touched a fragment of white frosting to his mouth.

Everyone was very quiet.

"Criminy, Doug!" Bo hissed as he pulled Doug

away from the wheelchair. "Why'd you do that? Is it Armistice Day? You gonna let me rip off your epaulettes? Why'd you give that cake to that awful old gink?"

Because, Douglas thought but didn't say, *because, well, I could hear him* breathe.

CHAPTER

Thirty-One

I'VE LOST, THOUGHT QUARTERMAIN. *I'VE LOST the game. Check. Mate.*

Bleak pushed Quartermain in his wheelchair, like a load of dried apricots and yellow wicker, around the block under the dying afternoon sun. He hated the tears that brimmed in his eyes.

"My God!" he cried. "What happened?"

Bleak said he wasn't sure whether it was a significant loss or a small victory.

"Don't small victory *me!*" Quartermain shouted.

"All right," said Bleak. "I won't."

"All of a sudden," said Quartermain, "in the boy's—"

He stopped, for he could not breathe.

"Face," he continued. "In the boy's face." Quartermain touched his mouth with his hands to pull the words out. He had seen *himself* peer forth from the boy's eyes, as if from an opened door. "How did *I* get in there, how?"

Bleak said nothing, but pushed Quartermain on through sun and shadow, quietly.

Quartermain did not touch the hand-wheels of his moving chair. He slumped, staring rigidly beyond the moving trees, the flowing white river of sidewalk.

"What *happened*?"

"If you don't know," said Bleak, "I won't tell you."

"I thought I'd defeated them. I thought I was mean and smart and clever. But I didn't win."

"No," said Bleak.

"I don't understand. Everything was set *up* for me to win."

"You did them a favor. You made them put one foot in front of the other."

"Is that what I did? So it's their victory."

"They might not know it, but yes. Every time you take a step, even when you don't want to," said Bleak. "When it hurts, when it means you rub chins with death, or even if it means dying, that's good. Anything that moves ahead, wins. No chess game was ever won by the player who sat for a lifetime thinking over his next move."

Quartermain let himself be pushed another block in silence and then said: "Braling was a fool."

"The metronome? Yes." Bleak shook his head. "He might be alive today if he hadn't scared himself to death. He thought he could stand still or even run backward. He thought he could trick life. Tricked himself right into a fine oration and a quick burial."

They turned a corner.

"Oh, it's hard to let go," said Quartermain. "All my life I've held on to everything I ever touched. Preach to me, Bleak!"

Bleak, obediently, preached: "Learning to *let go* should be learned before learning to *get*. Life should be touched, not strangled. You've got to relax, let it happen at times, and at others move forward with it. It's like boats. You keep your motor on so you can steer with the current. And when you hear the sound of the waterfall coming nearer and nearer, tidy up the boat, put on your best tie and hat, and smoke a cigar right up till the moment you go over. That's a triumph. Don't argue with the cataract."

"Take me around the block again."

"Here we go."

The leaf-light flickered on the paper-thin skin of the old men's wrists, the shadows alternating with fading sunlight. They moved in a soft whisper.

"All of a sudden. In that boy's face . . . He gave me a piece of cake, Bleak."

"I saw him."

"Why, why did he do it? He kept looking at me as if I were someone new. Was that it? Or what? Why did he do it? And there I was, me, staring out of his face. And I knew I'd lost."

"Let's say you didn't win, maybe. But you didn't lose."

"What broke me down all of a sudden? I hated that monster, and then, suddenly, I hated *myself.* Why?"

"Because he wasn't your son."

"Ridiculous!"

"Nevertheless. You never got married that I knew . . ."

"Never!"

"Never had children?"

"Never!"

"And the children never had children."

"Of course not. Impossible!"

"You cut yourself off from life. The boy has *reconnected* you. He is the grandson you should have had, to keep the juices flowing, life staying alert."

"Hard to believe."

"You're coming around. You can't cut all the phone lines and still be on speaking terms with the world. Instead of living inside your son and your son's son, you were *really* heading for the junkyard. The boy reminded you of your utter and complete finish."

"No more, no more!" Quartermain grabbed the hard rubber wheels of his chair, causing them to stop short.

"Face up to it," Bleak said. "We're both dumb old fools. A little late for wisdom, but better an ironic recognition than none at all."

Uncurling his friend's fingers from the spider web wheels, Bleak pushed the chair around a corner so the light of the dying sun stained their faces a healthy red, and added, "Look, life gives us everything. Then it takes it away. Youth, love, happiness, friends. Darkness gets it all in the end. We didn't have enough sense to know you can will it—life—to others. Your looks, your youth. Pass it on. Give it away. It's lent to us for only a while. Use it, let go without crying. It's a very fancy relay race, heading God knows where. Except now, in your last lap of the race, you find no one waiting for you on the track ahead. Nobody for you to hand the stick to. You've run the race for no reason. You've failed the team."

"Is that what I've done?"

"Yes. You weren't hurting the boy. Actually, what you were trying to do was make him grow up. You were both wrong for a while. Now you're both winning. Not because you want to, but because you have to."

"No, it's only he who's ahead. The idea was to grow them as fruit for the grave. But all I did was give them—"

"Love," said Bleak.

Quartermain could not say the word. That dreadful sweet, candy-sickening word. So trite, so true, so irritating, so wonderful, so frightening, and, in the end, so lost to himself.

"They won. I did them a favor, my God, a favor! I was blind! I wanted them to race about, like we run about, and wither, and be shocked by their withering, and die, like I'm dying. But they don't realize, they don't know, they're even happier, if that's possible."

"Yes." Bleak pushed the chair. "Happier. Because growing old isn't all that bad. None of it is bad if you have one thing. If you have the one thing that makes it all all right."

That dreadful word again!

"Don't say it!"

"But I'm thinking it," said Bleak, trying mightily to keep an unaccustomed smile from creasing his lips.

"So you're right, so I'm miserable, and here I sit, crying like a goddamn idiot fool!"

The freckled leaf-shadows passed over his liver-spotted hands. They fitted, for a moment, like a jigsaw and made his hands look muscled, tanned, and young. He stared at them, as if delivered free of age and corruption. Then the freckling, twinkling motion of passing trees went on.

"What do I do now, what do I do? Help me, Bleak."

"We can help ourselves. You were heading for the cliff. I tried to warn you. You can't hold them back now. If you'd had any sense, you might have encouraged the children to continue their damned revolution, never grow up, to be ego-centrics. Then they really would have been un-happy!"

"A fine time to tell me."

"I'm glad I didn't think of it. The worst thing is never to grow up. I see it all around. I see children in every house. Look there, that's Leonora's house, poor woman. And here's where those two old maids live, and their Green Machine. Children, children without love. And over there, take a look. There's the ravine. The Lonely One. There's a life for you, there's a child in a man's body. That's the ticket. You could make Lonely Ones of them all, given time and patience. You used the wrong strategy. Don't force people to grow. Baby them. Teach them to nurse their grievances and grow their private poison gardens. Little patches of hate and prejudice. If you wanted them unhappy, how much better to say, 'Revolt, I'm with you, charge! Ignorance, I'm for you! Down with the slob and the swine forever!'"

"Don't rub it in. I don't hate them anymore, anyway. What a strange afternoon, how odd. There I was, in his face. There I was, in love with the girl. It was as if time had never passed. I saw Liza again."

"It's still possible, of course, you can reverse the process. The child is in us all. It's not hard to keep the child locked there forever. Give it another try."

"No, I'm done with it. I'm done with wars. Let them go. If they can earn a better life than I did, let them earn it. I wouldn't be so cruel as to wish them my life now. I was in his face, remember, and I saw her. God, what a beautiful face! Suddenly I felt so young. Now, turn me around and roll me home. I want to think about the next year or so. I'll have to start figuring."

"Yes, Ebenezer."

"No, not Ebenezer, not Scrooge. I'm not anything. I haven't decided to be anything. You can't be anything that quickly. All I know is I'm not quite the same. I've got to figure what I want to be."

"You could give to charity."

"You know me better than that."

"You've got a brother."

"Lives in California."

"How long's it been since you've seen him?"

"Oh, God, thirty years."

"He has children, right?"

"Yes, I think so. Two girls and a boy. Grown now. Got children of their own."

"You could write a letter."

"What kind?"

"Invite them for a visit. You've got a big house. And one of those children, God help them, might seem like you. It struck me, if you can't have any private sense of destiny, immortality, you name it—you could get it secondhand from your brother's house. Seems to me you'd want to connect up with a thing like that."

"Foolish."

"No, common sense. You're too old for marriage and children, too old for everything except experiments. You know how things work. Some children look like their fathers, or mothers, or grandfathers, and some take after a distant brother. Don't you think you'd get a kick out of something like that?"

"Too easy."

"Think on it, anyway. Don't wait, or you'll sink back into being nothing but a mean old son-of-a-bitch again."

"So that's what I've been! Well, well. I didn't start out intending to be mean, but I got there somehow. Are *you* mean, Bleak?"

"No, because I know what I did to myself. I'm only mean in private. I don't blame others for my own mistakes. I'm bad in a different way than you, of course, with a sense of humor developed out of necessity." For a moment, Bleak's eyes seemed to twinkle, but maybe it was only the passing sun.

"I'll need a sense of humor from here on out. Bleak, visit me more often." Quartermain's gnarled fingers grasped Bleak's hand.

"Why would I visit you, you sorry old bastard, ever again?"

"Because we're the Grand Army, aren't we? You must help me think."

"The blind leading the sick," said Bleak. "Here we are."

He paused at the walk leading up to the gray, flake-painted house.

"Is that my place?" said Quartermain. "My God, it's ugly, ugly as sin. Needs paint."

"You can think about that, too."

"My God, what a Christ-awful ugly house! Wheel me in, Bleak."

And Bleak wheeled his friend up the walk toward his house.

CHAPTER

Thirty-Two

DOUGLAS STOOD WITH TOM AND CHARLIE IN the moist-smelling warm late-summer-green ravine. Mosquitoes danced their delicate dances upon the silence. A dancing idiot hum-tune.

"Everyone's gone," said Tom.

Douglas sat on a rock and took off his shoes.

"Bang, you're dead," said Tom, quietly.

"I wish I was, oh, I wish I was dead," said Doug.

Tom said, "Is the war over? Shall I take down the flag?"

"What flag?"

"Just the flag, that's all."

"Yeah. Take it down. But I'm not sure if the war is really over yet . . . but it sure has changed. I've just got to figure out how."

Charlie said, "Yeah, well, you did give *cake* to the enemy. If that wasn't the strangest thing . . ."

"Ta-ta-tahhhh," hummed Tom. He made furling motions in the warm empty silent air. He stood solemnly by the quiet creek in the summer evening with the sun fading. "Ta-ta-tahhhh. Ta-ta-tahhhh." He hummed "Taps." A tear fell off his cheek.

"Oh, for gosh sakes!" cried Douglas. "Stop!"

Douglas and Tom and Charlie climbed out of the ravine, and walked through the boxed and packaged town, through the avenues and streets and alleys, among the thousand-celled houses, the bright prisons, down the definite sidewalks and the positive lanes, and the country seemed far away and it was as if a sea had moved away from the shore of their life in one day. Suddenly there was the town and their lives to be lived in that town in the next forty years, opening and shutting doors and raising and lowering shades, and the green meadow was distant and alien.

Douglas looked over at Tom getting taller every minute, it seemed. He felt the hunger in his stomach and he thought of the miraculous foods at home and he thought of Lisabell blowing out the candles and sitting there with fourteen years burnt behind her and not caring, very pretty and solemn and beautiful. He thought of the Lonely One, very lonely indeed, wanting love, and now gone.

Douglas stopped at Charlie's house, feeling the season change about them.

"Here's where I leave you guys," said Charlie. "See you later, at the haunted house with those dumb girls."

"Yeah, see you later, Charlie."

"So long, Charlie," said Tom.

"You know something," said Charlie, turning back toward his friends, as if he'd suddenly re- membered something important. "I been thinkin'. I got an uncle, twenty-five years old. Came by earlier today in a big Buick, with his wife. A really nice, pretty lady. I was thinkin' all morning: Maybe I'll *let* them make me twenty-five. Twenty- five strikes me as a nice medium age. If they'll let me ride in a Buick with a pretty lady like that, I'll go along with them. But that's *it,* mind! No kids. It stops at squalling kids. Just a nice car and a pretty lady with me, ridin' along out toward the lake. Boy! I'll take about thirty years of that. I'm puttin' in my order for thirty years of being twenty-five. Fill 'er up and I'm on my way."

"It's something to think about," said Douglas.

"I'm goin' in the house to think about it right now," said Charlie.

"So, when do we start the war again?" said Tom.

Charlie and Douglas looked at each other.

"Heck, I dunno," said Doug, a little uncomfortably.

"Tomorrow, next week, next month?"

"I *guess.*"

"We *can't* give up the war!" said Tom.

"Heck, we're not giving it up," said Charlie. "Every *once* in a while we'll do it again, huh, Doug?"

"Oh, sure, sure!"

"Shift the strategy, identify new objectives, you know," said Charlie. "Oh, we'll have wars okay, Tom, don't you worry."

"Promise?" cried Tom, tears in his eyes.

"Cross our hearts, mother's honor."

"Okay," said Tom, lower lip trembling.

The wind whistled, was cool: it was an early autumn evening, no longer a late summer one.

"Well," said Charlie, standing there, smiling shyly, looking up from under his eyebrows at Doug. "It sure was a farewell summer, huh?"

"Sure was."

"Sure kept us busy."

"Sure did."

"Only thing is," said Tom, "it didn't come out in the papers: Who *won*?"

Charlie and Douglas stared at the younger boy.

"Who won? Don't be silly!" Douglas lapsed into silence, staring up into the sky. Then he fixed them with a stare. "I don't know. Us, them."

Charlie scratched inside his left ear. "Everybody. The first war in history where everybody won. I can't figure it. So long." He went on up the sidewalk, crossed the front yard, opened the door of his house, waved, and was gone.

"There goes Charlie," said Douglas.

"Boy, am I sad!" said Tom.

"About what?"

"I don't know. I keep playin' 'Taps' inside my head. It's a sad song, that's all."

"Don't start bawlin' now!"

"No, I'm just gonna be quiet. You know why? I guess I got it figured."

"Why?"

"Ice cream cones don't last."

"That's a silly thing to say."

"Ice cream cones are always gettin' done with. Seems I'm no sooner bitin' the top than I'm eatin' the tail. Seems I'm no sooner jumpin' in the lake at the start of vacation than I'm creepin' out the far side, on the way back to school. Boy, no wonder I feel bad."

"It's all how you look at it," said Doug. "My gosh, think of all the things you haven't even *started* yet. There's a million ice cream cones up ahead and ten billion apple pies and hundreds of summer vacations. Billions of things waitin' to be bit or swallowed or jumped in."

"Just once, though," said Tom, "I'd like one thing. An ice cream cone so big you could just keep eatin' and there isn't any end and you just go on bein' happy with it forever. Wow!"

"There's no such ice cream cone."

"Just *one* thing like that is all I ask," said Tom. "One vacation that never has a last day. Or one matinee with Buck Jones, boy, just ridin' along forever, bangin', and Indians fallin' like pop bottles. Gimme just one thing with no tail-end and I'd go *crazy*. Sometimes I just sit in the movie theater and cry when it says 'The End' for Jack Hoxie or Ken Maynard. And there's nothin' so sad as the last piece of popcorn at the bottom of the box."

"You better watch out," said Doug. "You'll be workin' yourself into another fit any minute. Just remember, darn it, there're ten thousand matinees waitin' right on up ahead."

"Well, here we are, home. Did we do anything today we might get licked for?"

"Nope."

"Then let's go in."

They did, slamming the door as they went.

CHAPTER

Thirty-Three

THE HOUSE STOOD ON THE EDGE OF THE RAVINE. It looked haunted, just like everyone said it was.

Tom and Charlie and Bo followed Doug up the side of the ravine and stood in front of the strange house at nine o'clock at night. In the distance, the courthouse clock bonged off the hour.

"There it is," said Doug. He turned his head right and left, as if he was looking for something.

"What are we gonna do?" asked Tom.

"Well," said Bo, "is it haunted, like they said?"

"From what I've heard, at eight o'clock, no," said Doug. "And not at nine. But starting around ten, strange sounds start to come from the house. I think we should hang around and find out. Besides, Lisabell said that she and her friends were going to be here. Let's wait and see."

They stood by some bushes by the front porch steps and they waited and at last the moon came up.

There was a sound of footsteps along the path somewhere and from inside the house, the sounds of someone going up some stairs.

Doug stood alert, craned his neck, but he couldn't quite see what was going on.

"Heck," said Charlie at last. "What are we doing here? I'm gosh-awful bored. I got homework. I think I better head home."

"Hold on," said Doug. "Let's wait just a few more minutes."

They waited as the moon got higher. And then, a little after ten, as the last peals of the courthouse clock faded away on the night air, they heard the noises. From inside the house, faint at first, almost imperceptible, there came a sound of rustling and scraping, as if someone was shifting trunks from one room to another.

A few minutes later, they heard a sharp cry, and then another cry, and then a sort of whispering and rustling and, finally, a dull thump.

"Those," said Doug, "were definitely ghost sounds. Like someone getting killed and the bodies being dragged around the rooms. Doesn't it sound like that?"

"Heck," said Tom, "I don't know."

"Don't ask me," said Bo.

"Well," said Charlie, "it's sure a god-awful racket. If there's another scream, I'm getting out of here."

They stood alert and waited, almost not breathing. Silence. And then, suddenly, more groans and cries and then something that sounded like a weak cry, "Help."

Then it faded away.

"That's it," said Charlie. "I've had enough."

"Me too," said Bo.

The two boys turned tail and ran.

There was a great whispering and the hair stood up on the back of Doug's neck.

"I don't know about you," said Tom, "but I'm gettin' out of here. If you want to stay to listen to some darned ghosts, you can, but not me. I'll see you at home, Doug."

Tom turned and ran.

Alone, Doug stood for a long while staring at the old house. Then he heard someone coming up the path behind him. He turned, his fists clenched, ready to defend himself against the midnight assailant.

"Lisabell," he said. "What are you doing here?"

"I *told* you I'd be here. But what are *you* doing here? I thought you were a scaredy-cat. Is it true what they say? Did you find out anything? I mean, it's all darn foolishness, isn't it? There's no such thing as ghosts, is there? That place can't be haunted."

"We thought," said Doug, "we'd come here and wait and see. But the others got scared and left and now it's only me. So I'm just standing here, waiting, listening."

They listened. A low cry wafted out of the house into the night air.

Lisabell said, "Is that a ghost?"

Doug strained to listen. "Yes, that's one."

A moment later they heard another great whisper and cry.

"Is that another?"

Doug looked at her face and said, "You look like you're enjoying this."

"I don't know," said Lisabell. "It's kind of strange, but the more I hear, I —" And here she smiled a strange smile. The whispers and the cries and murmurs from the house grew louder and Doug felt his whole body turn hot and then cold and then warm again.

Finally he reached down and found a large stone by the front of the house, reared his hand back, and flung it through the glass panes of the front door.

The glass exploded with a loud crash and the door creaked open, slowly. Suddenly, all the ghosts wailed at the same moment.

"Doug!" cried Lisabell. "Why did you do that?"

"Because . . ." said Doug.

And then it happened.

There was a rush of feet, a torrent of whispers, and a swirling mob of white shapes burst out of the house and down the stairs and along the path and away into the ravine.

"Doug," said Lisabell. "Why'd you do that?"

"Because," said Doug, "I couldn't stand it anymore. Someone had to scare *them* out. Someone had to act like they knew what they were doing. I bet they won't come back."

"That's terrible," said Lisabell. "Why would you want ghosts not to be here?"

"Why would you think," said Doug, "that they had a right to be here? We don't even know who they were."

"Well," said Lisabell, angrily. "Just for that I'm going to teach you a lesson."

"What?" said Douglas.

And Lisabell stepped up to him, grabbed him by the ears, and planted an immense kiss on Douglas's mouth. It lasted only an instant, but it was a blow like a bolt of lightning that had come out of the air and struck his face and anguished his body.

He shook from head to toe, his fingers extended, and somehow he imagined sparks firing out of his fingertips. His eyelids jittered and a fantastic flow of sweat broke out on his brow. He gasped and could not breathe.

Lisabell stood back, surveying her creation: Douglas Spaulding, hit by lightning.

Douglas fell back, afraid that she might touch him again. She laughed, her face merry.

"So there!" she cried. "That'll fix you."

She turned and ran away and left him in the invisible rain, a terrible storm, shaken, his whole body now hot, now cold, his jaw dropped, his lips trembling.

The explosion of the lightning bolt hit him again in memory, even stronger than when it had first struck.

Slowly, Doug felt himself sink to his knees, his head shaking, his mind wondering at what had happened and where Lisabell had gone.

He looked up at the now truly empty house. He wondered if he should go up the stairs and find out if maybe he hadn't just come out of the house himself.

"Tom," he whispered. "Take me home." And then he remembered: Tom wasn't there.

He turned, stumbled, almost fell down into the ravine, and tried to find his way home.

CHAPTER
Thirty-Four

QUARTERMAIN WOKE LAUGHING.

He lay wondering what in god-awful hell had *made* him happy. What was the dream, gone now, but so wondrous that it cracked his face and uncorked something resembling a chuckle beneath his ribs!? Holy Jesus. *What?*

In the dark he dialed Bleak.

"Do you know what time it is?" Bleak cried. "There's only one thing you ever wait half the night to churn my guts with—your stupid war. I thought you said the damned thing was over!"

"It is, it is."

"It is *what*?" shouted Bleak.

"Over," said Quartermain. "There are just a few more things I want to make sure of. It's what you would call the joyful aftermath. Bleak, remember the collection of oddities and medical freaks we put together one summer for a town fair, all those years ago? Do you think we could find those jars? Are they up in an attic or down in a basement somewhere?"

"I suppose so. But why?"

"Find them. Unlock them. We're bringing them out in the open again. Gather our army of gray. We have work to do. It's time."

Click. Hummm.

CHAPTER

Thirty-Five

A HUGE QUESTION MARK, PAINTED ON A PLY-wood shingle, hung over the tent entryway. The tent had been erected on one side of the lake-front grounds, and the entrance gave way into the darkness of a haphazardly constructed ply-wood lean-to museum. Inside was a series of platforms on which were no freaks, no beasts, no magicians, no people. Somehow, overnight, this mystery tent had appeared, as if it had pitched itself.

Across town, Quartermain smiled.

That morning, in school, Doug had found an unsigned handwritten note in his desk. Its message was simple, written with black ink in large block letters: "THE MYSTERY OF LIFE EXPLAINED. ? ? ? AT THE LAKEFRONT. LIMITED TIME ONLY." Doug passed the note among his friends, and as soon as school let out for the day, the boys had rushed down here, as fast as their feet could carry them. Now, entering the question mark tent with his friends, Doug was incredibly disappointed. *Migawd, no bones, no dinosaurs, no mad generals at war,* he thought. Nothing but night-dark canvas and flat platforms and . . . Douglas peered. Charlie squinted. Will, Bo, and Tom came last into the smell of old wood and tar-paper. There wasn't even a curator with a tall hat and baton to guide them along. There was only—

On top of a series of small tables were a number of large one- and two-gallon jars filled to the brim with a thick, clear liquid. Each jar was topped by a glass lid, and each lid had a red number on it—twelve in all—each number, painted in a shaky hand. And inside each of the jars . . . maybe that was it, at last, the things implied by the huge question mark outside.

"Heck," muttered Bo. "There's nothing here. What a gyp. So long, you guys."

And Bo turned, pushed the tent flap aside, and left.

"Wait," said Douglas, but Bo was already gone. "Tom, Charlie, Will, you won't leave, will you? You'll miss out if you go."

"But there's nothing here, just some old jars."

"Wait," said Doug. "It's *more* than just jars. What's *in* the jars? C'mon. Let's look closer."

They edged up to the platform and crept along, staring into the jars, one after another. There were no labels to tell them what they were looking at, just glass and liquid and a soft light that seemed to pulse within the liquid and shone on their eager, sweaty faces.

"What *is* that stuff in there?" asked Tom.

"Gosh knows. Look close."

Their eyes moved along, darted and stayed, stayed and darted, fastened and examined until their noses dilated and their mouths gaped.

"What's that, Doug? And that? And that one there?"

"How do *I* know? Move!" Doug went back to the beginning of the row and crouched down in front of the first jar so his eyes were level with whatever was inside it.

The big bright glass jar held what looked like a giant cold gray oyster. Doug peered at it, mumbled something to himself, then stood up and moved on. The boys followed.

Suspended within the liquid in the next jar was something that looked like a bit of translucent seaweed or, no, more like a seahorse, a miniature seahorse, sure!

And the glass jar after that held something that resembled a skinned rabbit or a raw cat with its fur shucked, getting bigger . . .

The boys' eyes moved, darted, stayed, flicked back to examine the first, second, third, fourth jars again.

"What's in *this* one, Doug?"

Five, six, seven.

"Look!"

They all looked and it might have been another animal, a squirrel or a monkey—sure, a monkey—but with transparent skin and a strange sorrowful expression.

Eight, nine, ten, eleven—the jars were numbered but had no names. There was nothing to hint at what the boys were looking at, what it was that froze their veins and iced their blood. Until at last, at the far end of the row, near the exit sign, they reached the last jar and all leaned toward it and blinked.

"That *can't* be!"

"Naw."

"It *is*," gasped Douglas. "A baby!"

"What's it *doing* in there?"

"Being dead, dummy."

"Yeah, but . . . how . . . ?"

All their eyes swiveled to rush back—eleven, ten, nine, eight, seven, six, five and four and three and two and one—to the first jar, the one holding the pale little oyster curlicue.

"If that's a baby . . ."

"Then," said Will, all numbness, "what in blazes are all those creepy things in the *other* jars?"

Douglas counted backward, then forward again, but stayed silent, his icy flesh all goose bumps.

"I got nothing to say."

"Upchuck, Doug, upchuck."

"Those things in the jars . . ." Doug began, face

pale, voice paler. "They're—they're babies, too!"

It was as if half a dozen sledgehammers had slammed into half a dozen stomachs.

"Don't *look* like babies!"

"Things from another world, maybe."

Another world, thought Douglas. *In those jars, drowned. Another world.*

"Jellyfish," Charlie said. "Squids. *You* know."

I know, thought Douglas. *Undersea.*

"It's got blue eyes," Will whispered. "It's looking at us."

"No, it's not," said Doug. "It's drowned."

"C'mon, Doug," Tom whispered. "I got the willies."

"Willies, heck," Charlie said. "I got the heebie-jeebies. Where'd all this stuff come from?"

"I don't know," Douglas said, chafing his elbows.

"The wax museum last year. That was sort of like this."

"These aren't wax," said Tom. "Oh, gosh, Doug, that's a real baby there, used to be alive. I never seen a dead baby before. I'm gonna be sick."

"Run outside. Go on!"

Tom turned and ran. In a moment, Charlie backed off and followed, his eyes darting from the baby to the jellyfish or whatever it was and then to the seahorse or what might be someone's earlobes, tympanum and all.

"How come there's no one here to tell us what all this stuff is?" Will wondered.

"Maybe," said Doug slowly, "maybe they're afraid to tell, or *can't* tell, or *won't*."

"Lord," said Will. "I'm froze."

From outside the tent's canvas walls came the sounds of Tom being sick.

"Hey!" Will cried suddenly. "It moved!"

Doug reached his hand out to the glass. "No, it didn't."

"It moved, darn it. It doesn't like us staring at it! Moved, I'm telling you! That's enough for me. So long, Doug."

And Doug was left alone in the dark tent with the cold glass jars holding the blind things that stared out with eyes that seemed to say how awful it was to be dead.

There's nobody to ask, thought Douglas, *no one here. No one to ask and no one to tell. How do we find out? Will we ever know?*

From the far end of the tent museum came the sound of high-pitched laughter. Six girls ran into the tent, giggling, letting in a bright wedge of sunlight.

Once the tent flap closed they stopped laughing, enveloped suddenly in darkness.

Doug turned blindly and walked out into the light.

He took a deep breath of the hot summer-like air, and squeezed his eyes shut. He could still see the platforms and the tables and the glass jars filled with thick fluid, and in the fluid, suspended, strange bits of tissue, alien forms from far unknown territories. What could be a swamp water creature with half an eye and half a limb, he knew, was not. What could be a fragment of ghost, of a spiritual upchuck come out of a fogbound book in a night library, was not. What could be the stillborn discharge of a favorite dog was not. In his mind's eye the things in the jars seemed to melt, from fluid to fluid, light to light. If you flicked your eyes from jar to jar, you could almost snap them to life, as if you were running bits of film over your eyeballs so that the tiny things became large and then larger, shaping

themselves into fingers, hands, palms, wrists, elbows, until finally, asleep, the last shape opened
wide its dull, blue, lashless eyes and fixed you
with its gaze that cried, *Look! See! I am trapped
here forever! What am I? What is the question,
what, what? Could it be, you there, below, outside looking in, could it be that I am . . . you?*

Beside him, rooted to the grass, stood Charlie
and Will and Tom.

"What was *that* all about?" Will whispered.

"I almost—" Doug started but Tom inter-
rupted, tears running down his cheeks.

"How come I'm crying?"

"Why would anyone be crying?" said Will,
but his eyes were wet, too. "Darn," he whispered.

They heard a creaking sound. From the corner
of his eye, Douglas saw a woman go by pushing a
carriage in which something struggled and cried.

Beyond in the afternoon crowd, a pretty
woman walked arm in arm with a sailor. Down
by the lake a mob of girls played tag, hair flying,
leaping, bounding, measuring the sand with
swift feet. The girls ran away down the shore
and Douglas, hearing their laughter, turned his

gaze back to the tent, the entry, and the large strange question mark.

Douglas started to move back toward the tent, like a sleepwalker.

"Doug?" said Tom. "Where you going? You going back in to look at all that junk again?"

"Maybe."

"Why?" exploded Will. "Creepy-looking stuff that someone stuck in old pickle jars. I'm going home. C'mon."

"You go on," said Doug.

"Besides," said Will, passing a hand across his forehead, "I don't feel so good. Maybe I'm scared. How about you?"

"What's to be scared of?" said Tom. "Like you said, it's just some creepy old stuff."

"See you later, guys." Doug walked slowly to the entryway and stopped in the shadows. "Tom, wait for me." Doug vanished.

"Doug!" Tom cried, face pale, shouting into the tent at the tables and jars and alien creatures. "Be *careful,* Doug. Watch *out!*"

He started to follow but stopped, shivering, clutching his elbows, gritting his teeth, half in, half out of night, half in, half out of sun.

III.

APPOMATTOX

CHAPTER
Thirty-Six

SUDDENLY THE TOWN WAS FULL OF GIRLS, GIRLS
running here, walking there, going in doors,
coming out, girls in the dime store, girls dangling
their legs at the soda fountain, girls in mirrors or
reflected in windows, stepping off curbs or stepping up, and all of them, all in bright not yet fall,
not quite autumn dresses, and all, well maybe
not all but almost all, with wind blowing their
hair and all with downcast eyes looking to see
where their shoes might take them.

It seemed to happen overnight, this infestation

of girls, and Douglas walked through the town as if it were a mirror maze, walked down to the ravine steps and halfway up the jungle path before he realized where he was. From the top of the last rise he could almost see the lake and the sand and the tent with the question mark over the entrance.

He kept walking and found himself, inexplicably, in Mr. Quartermain's front yard, waiting for he couldn't say what.

Quartermain, half-hidden in shadow on the front porch, leaned forward in his rocking chair, creaking the wicker, creaking his bones. For a long moment the old man looked one way, the boy another, until their gazes locked.

"Douglas Spaulding?" Quartermain said.

"Mr. Quartermain?" asked the boy.

It was as if they were meeting for the first time.

"Douglas Spaulding." This time it was not a question, but a confirmation. "Douglas Hinkston Spaulding."

"Sir." And this was not a question from the boy, either. "Mr. Calvin C. Quartermain." And again, "Sir."

"What're you doing down there, so far out on the lawn?"

Douglas was surprised. "Dunno."

"Why don't you come up here?" said Quartermain.

"I've got to get home," said Douglas.

"No hurry. Why don't we sort out the sic transits, letting loose the dogs of war, havocs cried, all *that*."

Douglas almost laughed, but found he could not take the first step.

"Look," said Quartermain. "If I take out my teeth I won't bite." He pantomimed as if removing something from his mouth but stopped, for Douglas was on the first step, and then the second, and finally at the top, where the old man nodded at another rocker.

Whereupon a remarkable thing took place.

Even as Douglas sat it seemed that the porch planks sank the merest half inch under his weight.

Simultaneously, Mr. Quartermain felt his wicker seat move *up* half an inch!

Then, still further, as Quartermain settled back in his rocker, the porch sank under him.

And at that precise moment, the chair under Douglas rose silently, a quarter inch.

So that each, only sensing, only half knowing,

felt that he occupied one end of an invisible teeter-totter which, as they spoke quietly, moved up, moved down, first Douglas sinking as Quartermain rose, then Quartermain descending as Douglas imperceptibly lifted—now one up, now down; now the other up, now down; slowly, slowly.

Now Quartermain high in the soft air of the dying summer, a moment later, Douglas the same.

"Sir?"

"Yes, son?"

He's never called me that before, thought Douglas, and looked at the old man's face softened with some half-perceived sympathy.

Quartermain leaned forward.

"Before you ask me whatever you've got on your mind, let me ask you something."

"Sir?"

The old man's voice was quiet.

"How old are you?"

Doug felt the breath sift over his lips.

"Ummm, eighty-one?"

"What?!"

"I dunno. I mean. I dunno."

At last Douglas added, "And *you,* sir?"

"Well, now," said Quartermain.

"Sir?"

"Well, let me see. Twelve?"

"Sir?!"

"Or maybe thirteen would be better?"

"*Yes,* sir."

Teeter up, teeter down.

"Douglas," said Quartermain at last, "I'd like you to tell me. What's life all about?"

"My gosh," cried Douglas, "I was going to ask *you* that very question!"

Quartermain pulled back.

"Let's rock awhile."

There was no motion up, no motion down. They held still.

"It's been a long summer," the old man said.

"Seemed like it would never end," Doug agreed.

"I don't think it has. Not yet," said Quartermain.

He reached out to the table beside him and found some lemonade and poured a glass and handed it over. Douglas held the glass and took a small sip. Quartermain cleared his throat and looked at his hands.

"Appomattox."

Douglas blinked. "Sir?"

Quartermain looked around at the railings, the boxes of geraniums, and the wicker rockers that he and the boy sat still in.

"Appomattox. You ever heard of that?"

"In school once."

"The thing is, which one is me, which one is you?"

"Which one what, sir?"

"Lee and Grant, Doug. Grant and Lee. What color uniform are you wearing?"

Douglas looked down at his sleeves and his pants and his shoes.

"I see you have no better answer than I do," observed Quartermain.

"No, sir."

"It was a long time ago. Two tired old generals. Appomattox."

"Yes, sir."

"Now." Cal Quartermain leaned forward so his wicker bones creaked. "What is it you want to know?"

"Everything," said Douglas.

"Everything?" Quartermain laughed gently. "That'll take at least ten minutes."

"How about something?" said Douglas finally.

"Something? One *special* thing? Why, Doug, *that* will take a lifetime. I've been at it a while. *Everything* rolls off my tongue, easy as pie. But *something*! *Something*! I get lockjaw just trying to define it. So let's talk about *everything* instead, for now. When you finally unhinge your tongue and find one special eternal *forever* thing of substance, let me know. Promise?"

"Promise."

"Now, where were we? Life? *There's* an *everything* topic. You want to know all about life?"

Douglas nodded, head ducked.

"Steel yourself."

Douglas looked up and fixed Quartermain with a stare like the sky and all of time waiting.

"Well, to begin . . ." He paused and held out his hand for Douglas's empty glass. "You're going to need this, son."

Quartermain poured. Douglas took and drank.

"Life," said the old man, and murmured, muttered, and murmured again.

CHAPTER
Thirty-Seven

CALVIN C. QUARTERMAIN WOKE BECAUSE SOME-
one had said something or called out in the night
air.

But that was impossible. Nobody or nothing
had.

He looked out the window at the great face of
the courthouse clock and could almost hear it
clearing its throat, preparing to announce three
in the morning.

"Who's there?" Quartermain said into the
cool night air.

Me.

"How's that again?" Quartermain lifted his head and peered left and right.

Me. Remember?

And now he looked down along the quilt.

Without moving his hands to touch and find, he knew his old friend was there. A bare subsistence of friend, but still, friend.

He did not lift his head to peer down along the sheets to the small mound there below his navel, between his legs. It was hardly more than a heartbeat, a pulse, a lost member, a ghost of flesh. But it was there.

"So you're back?" he said to the ceiling, and snorted a chopped-off laugh. "It's been a long while."

In reply, a soft pulse of recognition.

"How long will you stay?"

The slender mound beat its own private heart twice, three times, but showed no signs of going anywhere; it seemed it would stay awhile.

"Is this your very *last* visit?" asked Quartermain.

Who can say? was the silent reply of his old

friend revisiting, nested in a wirework of ancient hair.

I do not so much mind my scalp turning gray, Quartermain had once said, but when you find whiteness sprouting down *there*, to hell with it. Let the rest of me age, but not *that*!

But age he did and age *it* did. He was all of a dead winter grayness now. Still, there was this heartbeat, this tender and incredible pulse saluting him, a promise of spring, a seedbed of memory, a touch of . . . what was the word out there in the town in this strange weather when everyone's juices roused again?

Farewell summer.

Dear God, yes.

Don't go yet. Stay. I need a friend.

His friend stayed. And they talked. At three in the morning.

"Why do I feel so happy?" said Quartermain. "What's been going on? Was I mad? Am I cured? Is *this* the cure?" Quartermain's teeth chattered with an outrageous laugh.

I just came to say goodbye, the voice whispered.

"Goodbye?" Quarterman's laughter caught in his throat. "Does that mean—"

It does, came the whisper. *It's been a lot of years. It's time to move on.*

"Time, yes," said Quartermain, his eyes watering. "Where are you going?"

Can't say. You'll know when the time comes.

"How will I know?"

You'll see me. I'll be there.

"How will I know it's *you*?"

You'll know. You've always known everything, but me above all.

"You're not leaving town?"

No, no. I'll be around. But when you see me, don't embarrass anyone, all right?

"Of course."

The quilt and the sheets under the quilt were lowering, melting to rest. The whisper grew fainter.

"Wherever you go . . ." began Quartermain.

Yes?

"I wish you a long life, a good life, a happy one."

Thank you.

A pause. Silence. Quartermain found he didn't know what to say next.

Goodbye then?

The old man nodded, his eyes misted with tears.

His bed, the coverlet, his body was flat as a tabletop. What had been there for seventy years was now totally and completely gone.

"Goodbye," said Mr. Quartermain into the still night air.

I wonder, he thought, *where, oh just where in hell he has gone?*

The great courthouse clock struck three.

And Mr. Quartermain slept.

Douglas opened his eyes in the dark. The town clock finished the last stroke of three.

He looked at the ceiling. Nothing. He looked at the windows. Nothing. Only the night breeze fluttered the pale curtains.

"Who's there?" he whispered.

Nothing.

"Someone's here," he whispered.

And at last he asked again, "Who," he said, "is there?"

Here, something murmured.

"What?"

Me, something spoke in the night.

"Who's me?"

Here, was the quiet answer.

"Where?"

Here, quietly.

"Where?"

And Douglas looked all around and then down.

"There?"

Yes, oh, yes.

Down along his body, below his chest, below his navel, between his two hipbones, where his legs joined. There it was.

"Who *are* you?" he whispered.

You'll find out.

"Where did you come from?"

A billion years past. A billion years yet to come.

"That's no answer."

It's the only one.

"Were you . . ."

What?

"Were you down in that tent today?"

What?

"Inside. In those glass jars. *Were* you?"

In a way, yes.

"What do you mean, 'in a way'?"

Yes.

"I don't understand."

You will, when we get to know each other.

"What's your name?"

Give me one. We always have names. Every boy names us. Every man says that name ten thousand times in his life.

"I don't . . ."

Understand? Just lie there. You have two hearts now. Feel the pulse. One in your chest. And one below. Yes?

"Yes."

Do you actually feel the two hearts?

"Yes. Oh, yes!"

Go to sleep then.

"Will you be here when I wake up?"

Waiting for you. Awake long before you. Good night, friend.

"*Are* we? Friends?"
The best you ever had. For life.

There was a soft rabbit running. Something hit the bed, something burrowed beneath the blankets.

"Tom?"

"Yeah," said the voice from under the covers. "Can I sleep here tonight? Please!"

"*Why*, Tom?"

"I dunno. I just had this awful feeling tomorrow morning we'd find you gone or dead or both."

"I'm not going to die, Tom."

"Someday you will."

"Well . . ."

"Can I stay?"

"Okay."

"Hold my hand, Doug. Hold on tight."

"Why?"

"You ever think the Earth's spinning at twenty-five thousand miles per hour or something? It could throw you right off if you shut your eyes and forget to hold on."

"Give me your hand. There. Is that better?"

"Yeah. I can sleep now. You had me scared there for a while."

A moment of silence, breath going in and out.

"Tom?"

"Yeah?"

"You see? I didn't ditch you, after all."

"Thank gosh, Doug, oh, thank gosh."

A wind came up outside and shook all the trees and every leaf, every last one fell off and blew across the lawn.

"Summer's over, Tom."

Tom listened.

"Summer's done. Here comes autumn."

"Halloween."

"Boy, think of *that*!"

"I'm *thinking*."

They thought, they slept.

The town clock struck four.

And Grandma sat up in the dark and named the season just now over and done and past.

Afterword

THE IMPORTANCE OF BEING STARTLED

The way I write my novels can best be described as imagining that I'm going into the kitchen to fry a couple of eggs and then find myself cooking up a banquet. Starting with very simple things, they then word-associate themselves with further things until I'm up and running and eager to find out the next surprise, the next hour, the next day or the next week.

Farewell Summer began roughly fifty-five years ago when I was very young and had no knowledge of novels and no hope of creating a novel that was sensible. I had to wait for years for material to accumulate and take me, unaware, so that as I sat at my typewriter quite suddenly there would be bursts of surprise, resulting in short stories or longer narratives that I then connected together.

The main action of the novel takes place in a ravine that cut across my life. I lived on a short street in Waukegan, Illinois, and the ravine was immediately east of my home and ran on for several miles in two directions and then circled around to the north and to the south, and finally to the west. So, in effect, I lived on an island where I could, at any time, plunge into the ravine and have adventures.

There I imagined myself in Africa or on the planet Mars. That being so, and my going through the ravine every day on my way to school, and skating and sledding there in winter, this ravine remained central to my life and so it was natural that it would become the center of this novel, with all of my friends on both sides of the ravine and the old people who were curious time-pieces in my life.

I've always been fascinated by elderly people. They came and went in my life and I followed them and questioned them and learned from them, and that is primarily true in this novel because it is a novel about children and old people who are peculiar Time Machines.

Many of the greatest friendships in my lifetime have been with men or women who were in their eighties or nineties and I welcomed the chance to ask them questions and then to sit, very quietly, saying nothing and learning from their responses.

In a way, *Farewell Summer* is a novel about learning by encountering old people and daring to ask them certain questions and then sitting back and listening to their answers. The questions posed by Doug, and the answers given by Mr. Quartermain, provide the organization of the action of the chapters and the final resolution of the book.

The bottom line here is that *I* am not the one in control. I do not try to steer my characters; I let them live their lives and speak their truths as quickly as possible. I listen, and write them down.

Farewell Summer is actually an extension of my book *Dandelion Wine,* which I completed fifty-five years ago. When I delivered it to my publishers they said, "My God, this is much too long. Why don't we publish the first 90,000 words as a novel and keep the second part for some future year when you feel it is ready to be published." At the time, I called the full, primitive version *The Blue Remembered Hills.* The original title for what would become *Dandelion Wine* was *Summer Morning, Summer Night.* Even all those years ago, I had a title ready for this unborn book: *Farewell Summer.*

So, it has taken all these years for the second part of *Dandelion Wine* to evolve to a point where I felt it was correct to send it out into the world. During the ensuing years, I waited for those parts of the novel to attract further ideas and further metaphors to add richness to the text.

Surprise is everything with me. When I go to bed at night I give myself instructions to startle myself when I wake in the morning. That was one of the great adventures in letting this novel evolve: my instructions at night and my being startled in the morning by revelations.

The influence of my grandparents and my aunt, Neva Bradbury, is in evidence all through the narrative. My grandfather was a very wise and patient man, who knew the importance of showing, not simply telling. My grandmother was a wonderful woman who had an innate understanding of what made boys tick. And my aunt Neva was the guardian and gardener of the metaphors that became me. She saw to it that I was fed all the best fairy tales, poetry, cinema, and theater, so that I was continually in a fever about life and eager to write it all down. Today, all these years later, I still feel in the writing process that she is looking over my shoulder and beaming with pride.

Beyond that there is very little to add except that I'm glad that the long haul of writing this novel is finished and I hope that there is pleasure in it for everyone. It has been a great pleasure for me, to revisit my beloved Green Town—to gaze up at the haunted house, to hear the deep gongs of the courthouse clock, to run through the ravine, to be kissed by a girl for the first time, and to listen to and learn from the wisdom of those who have gone before.

Turn the page to discover
more classic masterworks
from Ray Bradbury,
"an author whose fanciful imagination,
poetic prose,
and mature understanding
of human character have
won him an international reputation."
—*New York Times*

NOVELS

Dandelion Wine

Twelve-year-old Douglas Spaulding knows Green Town, Illinois, is as vast and deep as the whole wide world that lies beyond the city limits. It is a pair of brand-new tennis shoes, the first harvest of dandelions for Grandfather's renowned intoxicant, the distant clang of the trolley's bell on a hazy afternoon. It is yesteryear and tomorrow blended into an unforgettable always.

But as young Douglas is about to discover, summer can be more than the repetition of established rituals whose mystical power holds time at bay. It can be a best friend moving away, a human time machine who can transport you back to the Civil War, or a sideshow automaton able to glimpse the bittersweet future. The author's most deeply personal work, *Dandelion*

Wine is a semi-autobiographical recollection of a magical small town summer in 1928—a priceless distillation of all that is eternal about boyhood and summer.

"[A] beautiful paean
to growing up in the Midwest."
—*St. Louis Post-Dispatch*

The Martian Chronicles

Mars is a place of hope, dreams and metaphor—of crystal pillars and fossil seas—where a fine dust settles on the great, empty cities of a silently destroyed civilization. It is here the invaders have come to despoil and commercialize, to grow and to learn, to escape a world with no future or promise of tomorrow. The Earthman conquers Mars . . . and then is conquered *by* it, lulled by dangerous lies of comfort and familiarity, and enchanted by the lingering glamour of an ancient, mysterious native race.

In his groundbreaking, provocatively imagined

chronicle of Earth's settlement of the fourth world from the sun, Bradbury stunningly exposes our strength, weakness, folly, and poignant humanity in a strange and breathtaking world where humanity does not belong.

"Thank the shades of Twain and Melville and the living presence of Pynchon . . . that this Poet Laureate of the Chimerical and Phantasmagoric is still with us, still writing, still freshening our ration of dream dust."
—*Los Angeles Times*

From the Dust Returned

They have lived for centuries in a house of legend and mystery in upper Illinois—and they are *not* like other Midwesterners. Rarely encountered in daylight hours, their children are curious and wild; their old ones have survived since before the Sphinx first sank its paws deep in Egyptian sands. And some sleep in beds with lids.

Now the house is being readied for the gala

homecoming that will gather together the far-flung branches of this odd and remarkable family. But in the midst of eager anticipation, a sense of doom pervades, for the world is changing. And death, no stranger, will always shadow this most singular family, and the boy who, more than anyone, carries the burden of time on his shoulders: Timothy, the sad and different foundling son who must share it all, remember, and tell . . . and who, alone out of all of them, must one day age and wither and die.

"Filled with poetic imagery, paeans to yesterday and lost faith, and plenty of magic storytelling, *From the Dust Returned* is ample proof that 81-year-old Bradbury hasn't lost the passion and fire of his youth. Like the members of his [Elliot] Family, Bradbury's talents are immortal."

—*Denver Post*

Something Wicked This Way Comes

The carnival rolls in sometime after the midnight hour of a chilly mid-western October eve. Young boyhood companions James Nightshade and Will Halloway are the first to heed its call. From a place of safety, they watch a midway come to spectral life, their emotions a riot of eagerness, trepidation, bravado, and uncertainty. For they can sense the change that's in the air; that this is the Autumn in which innocence must vanish in the harsh, acrid smoke of disillusionment . . . and horror.

In this season of dying, Cooger & Dark's Pandemonium Shadow Show has come to Green Town, Illinois, to destroy every life touched by its strange and sinister mystery. And two boys will discover the secret of its smoke, mazes, and mirrors; two friends who will soon know all too well the heavy cost of wishes . . . and the stuff of nightmare.

"Ray Bradbury is an old-fashioned romantic who's capable of imagining a dystopic future.

He can evoke nostalgia for a mythic,
golden past or raise goosebumps
with tales of horror."
—*Chicago Tribune*

A Graveyard for Lunatics

Halloween night, 1954. A young, film-obsessed scriptwriter has just been hired at one of the great studios. An anonymous invitation leads him from the giant Maximus Films backlot to an eerie graveyard separated from the studio by a single wall. There he makes a terrifying discovery that thrusts him into a maelstrom of intrigue and mystery—and into the dizzy exhilaration of the movie industry at the height of its glittering power.

Here are monocled directors, ham-handed studio heads, obsessive actors, fanatical devotees, and one glorious special effects genius—all part of the tarnished golden age of Tinseltown, all remembered with unmatched brilliance by the masterful Ray Bradbury.

Death Is a Lonely Business

Toiling away amid the looming palm trees and decaying bungalows, a struggling young writer spins fantastic stories from his fertile imagination upon his clacking typewriter. Trying not to miss his girlfriend (away studying in Mexico), the nameless writer steadily crafts his literary effort—until strange things begin happening around him.

From peculiar phone calls to odd clumps of seaweed on the doorstep, the mysterious incidents continue to escalate around the writer until his friends fall victim to a series of mysterious "accidents." Aided by Elmo Crumley, a savvy, street-smart detective, and a reclusive actress of yesteryear with an intense hunger for life, the wordsmith sets out to find the connection between the bizarre events, and in doing so, uncovers the truth about his own creative abilities.

"The protagonist is Bradbury himself, as a young writer and amateur sleuth . . . His pursuit of the killer stalking the neighborhood's old eccentrics obsessed with the past opens up their private world . . . This rampant nostalgia also applies to the author, who bestows on his younger self the ideas and insights that would grow into his classic stories."
—*Publishers Weekly*

Let's All Kill Constance

On a dismal evening in the previous century, an unnamed writer in Venice, California, answers a furious pounding at his beachfront bungalow door and again admits Constance Rattigan into his life. An aging, once-glamorous Hollywood star, Constance is running in fear from something she dares not acknowledge—and vanishes as suddenly as she appeared, leaving the narrator two macabre books: twin listings of the Tinseltown dead and soon to be dead, with Constance's name included among them.

And so begins an odyssey as dark as it is wondrous, as the writer sets off in a broken-down jalopy with his irascible sidekick Crumley to sift through the ashes of a bygone Hollywood—a graveyard of ghosts and secrets where each twisted road leads to grim shrines and shattered dreams . . . and, all too often, to death.

> "Ray Bradbury's writing remains as rich and ripe as ever."
> —*Washington Post Times-Herald*

Green Shadows, White Whale

In 1953, the brilliant but terrifying titan of cinema John Huston summons the young writer Ray Bradbury to Ireland. The apprehensive scribe's quest is to capture on paper the fiercest of all literary beasts—Moby Dick—in the form of a workable screenplay so the great director can begin filming.

But from the moment he sets foot on Irish soil, the author embarks on an unexpected odyssey. Meet congenial IRA terrorists, tippling men of the cloth, impish playwrights, and the boyos at Heeber Finn's pub. In a land where myth is reality, poetry is plentiful, and life's misfortunes are always cause for celebration, *Green Shadows, White Whale* is the grandest tour of Ireland you'll ever experience—with the irrepressible Ray Bradbury as your enthusiastic guide.

"A must for anyone enamored of the Celtic twilight in all its fanciful disguises."
—*Atlanta Journal Constitution*

SHORT FICTION

Bradbury Stories

In this landmark volume, America's preeminent storyteller offers us one hundred treasures from a lifetime of words and ideas. The stories within these pages were chosen by Bradbury himself, and span a career that blossomed in the pulp magazines of the early 1940s and continues to flourish in the new millennium. Here are representatives of the legendary author's finest works of short fiction, including many that have not been republished for decades, all forever fresh and vital, evocative and immensely entertaining.

"[A]ny Bradbury at all is supremely well worth a weekend's reading."
—*Ft. Lauderdale Sun-Sentinel*

The Cat's Pajamas

Ray Bradbury has once again pulled together a stellar group of stories sure to delight readers of all ages. In *The Cat's Pajamas* we are treated to a treasure trove of Bradbury gems old and new—eerie and strange, nostalgic and bittersweet, searching and speculative—all but two of which have never been published before. *The Cat's Pajamas* is a joyous celebration of the lifelong work of a literary legend.

"Some writers have a presence so pervasive that we take them wholly for granted; they're the floor we walk on. For almost 70 years no, ceaselessly, untiringly, Bradbury has toiled in his garden. . . . Ray Bradbury has accomplished what very few artists do. With his visions of possible futures and edgy presents, he has shown us a way out of the trap of our selves, shown us how we can break the momentum of the past, of our habits and willful ignorance.

He has not only transformed science fiction, he has changed us."
—*Boston Sunday Globe*

One More for the Road

Here is a rich elixir distilled from the pungent fruit of experience and imagination, expertly prepared by a superior mixologist. Taste the warm mysteries of summer and the bitterness of betrayed loves and abandoned places. This glass overflows with a heady brew that will set your mind spinning and carry you to remarkable locales: a house where time has no boundaries; a movie theater where deconstructed schlock is drunkenly reassembled into art; a faraway planet plagued by an epidemic of sorrow; a wheat field that hides a strangely welcome enemy. The comforts of arguments eternal; the addictive terror of a predawn phone call; the ghosts of dear friends, of errant sons and lost fathers, and of lovers both joyously remembered and never-to-be, are but a few of the ingredients that have gone into Bradbury's savory cocktail. And every satisfying swallow brings new surprises and revelations.

"Sci-fi fans and 35-year-old virgins alike revere Bradbury as one of the genre's last living masters . . . his collection of 25 new short stories ranks up there with classics such as *Fahrenheit 451*. . . . Bradbury is still boldly going where few writers have gone before."
—*Maxim*

Driving Blind

The incomparable Ray Bradbury is in the driver's seat, off on twenty-one unforgettable excursions through fantasy, time and memory, and there are surprises waiting around every curve and behind each mile marker. The journey promises to be a memorable one.

"A must . . . Bradbury returns in top form."
—*Library Journal*

Quicker Than the Eye

Twenty-one remarkable stories that run the gamut from total reality to light fantastic, from high noon to long after midnight. A true master tells all, revealing the strange secret of growing young and mad; opening a Witch Door that links two intolerant centuries; joining an ancient couple in their wild assassination games; celebrating life and dreams in the unique voice that has favored him across six decades and has enchanted millions of readers the world over.

> "Whimsical, fantastic and sometimes terrifying."
> —*Kansas City Star*

A Sound of Thunder and Other Stories

With his disarmingly simple style and complex imagination, Ray Bradbury has seized the minds of American readers for decades. This collection showcases thirty-two of Bradbury's most famous tales in which he lays bare the depths of the human soul. The thrilling title story, *A Sound of Thunder*, tells of a hunter sent on safari—sixty million years in the past. But all it takes is one wrong step in the prehistoric jungle to stamp out the life of a delicate and harmless butterfly—and possibly something else much closer to home . . .

"A powerful writing talent."
—*Fort Worth Star-Telegram*

A Medicine for Melancholy

Ray Bradbury is a painter who uses words rather than brushes—for he creates lasting visual images that, once observed, are impossible to forget. Sinister mushrooms growing in a dank cellar. A family's first glimpse at Martians. A wonderful white vanilla ice-cream summer suit that changes everyone who wears it. A great artist drawing in the sand on the beach. A clunky contraption made out of household implements to help some kids play a game called Invasion. The most marvelous Christmas display a little boy ever saw. All those images and many more are inside this book—timeless short fiction that ranges from the farthest reaches of space to the innermost stirrings of the heart.

"Bradbury has a style all his own, much imitated but never matched . . . After writing for more than fifty years, Bradbury has become more than pretty good at it. He has become a master."
—*Oregonian* (Portland)

The Illustrated Man

In this classic collection of tales, Bradbury's stories breathe and move—animated by sharp, intaken breath and flexing muscle. Here are eighteen startling visions of humankind's destiny, unfolding across a canvas of decorated skin—visions as keen as the tattooist's needle and as colorful as the inks that indelibly stain the body.

Ray Bradbury's *The Illustrated Man* is a kaleidoscopic blending of magic, imagination, and truth, widely believed to be one of the Grandmaster's premier accomplishments: as exhilarating as interplanetary travel, as maddening as a walk in a million-year rain, and as comforting as simple, familiar rituals on the last night of the world.

"A preeminent storyteller . . . An icon in American literature."
—*Virginian Pilot*

I Sing the Body Electric! and Other Stories

A wonder-filled carnival of delight and terror that stretches from the verdant Irish countryside to the coldest reaches of outer space, the stories that make up *I Sing the Body Electric!* are united by one common thread: a vivid and profound understanding of the vast set of emotions that bring strength and mythic resonance to our frail species.

A horrified mother may give birth to a strange blue pyramid. A man may take Abraham Lincoln out of the grave—and meet another who puts him back. An amazing Electrical Grandmother may come to live with a grieving family. An old parrot may have learned over long evenings to imitate the voice of Ernest Hemingway, and become the last link to the last link to the great man. A priest on Mars may confront his fondest dream: to meet the Messiah. Each of these magnificent creations has something to tell us about our own humanity—and all of their fates await you in twenty-eight classic Bradbury stories and one luscious poem.

> "His stories and novels are part of the American language."
> —*Washington Post*

The October Country

Welcome to a land Ray Bradbury calls "the Undiscovered Country" of his imagination—that vast territory of ideas, concepts, notions and conceits where the stories of this collection were born. Bradbury has spent many lifetimes in this remarkable place—strolling through empty, shadow-washed fields at midnight; exploring long-forgotten rooms gathering dust behind doors bolted years ago to keep strangers locked out . . . and secrets locked in. The nights are longer in this country. The cold hours of darkness move like autumn mists deeper and deeper toward winter. But the moonlight reveals great magic here—and a breathtaking vista.

The October Country is many places: a picturesque Mexican village where death is a tourist attraction; a city beneath the city where drowned lovers are silently reunited; a carnival midway where a tiny man's most cherished fantasy can be fulfilled night after night. Its inhabitants live, dream, work, die—and sometimes live again—discovering, often too late, the high price of citizenship. Here a glass jar can hold memories and nightmares; a woman's newborn child can plot murder; and a man's skeleton can war against him. Here there is no escaping the dark stranger who lives upstairs . . . or the reaper who wields the world. Each of these stories is a wonder, imagined by an acclaimed tale-teller writing from a place of shadows. But there is astonishing beauty in these shadows, born from a prose that enchants and enthralls.

"Bradbury has a light, almost ephemeral touch that belies the underlying depth of feeling in his writing."
—*BookPage*

NON-FICTON

Bradbury Speaks

On subjects as diverse as fiction, the future, film, famous personalities, and more, Ray Bradbury has much to say, as only he can say it. Collected within this volume are memories, ruminations, opinions, prophecies, and philosophies from one of the most influential and admired writers of our time. As unique, unabashed, and irrepressible as the artist himself, here is an intimate portrait, painted with the master's own words, of the one and only Ray Bradbury—far more revealing than any mere memoir, for it opens windows not only into his life and work but also into his mind and heart.

"By turns whimsical, insightful, and unabashedly metaphoric."
—*Booklist*

RAY BRADBURY

NOW AND FOREVER
978-0-06-113157-8

FAREWELL SUMMER
978-0-06-113155-4

LET'S ALL KILL CONSTANCE
978-0-06-056178-9

ONE MORE FOR THE ROAD
978-0-06-103203-5

FROM THE DUST RETURNED
978-0-380-78961-0

DRIVING BLIND
978-0-380-78960-3

SOMETHING WICKED THIS WAY COMES
978-0-380-72940-1

QUICKER THAN THE EYE
978-0-380-78959-7